SPIROU IN MOSCOW

FANTASY /ˈfæntəsi/ Noun (from Greek *phantasia*). A capricious or fantastic idea; a conceit. That which comes from one's imagination. For example: "Any resemblance to actual comrades, living or dead, is nothing but pure fantasy."

Script and artwork:
TOME – JANRY
Colours:
STEPHANE DE BECKER
Photograph:
YVAN MATHIEU

Originally published in 1990, this story harks back to a bygone era and its specific historical context. Anyone who would see in it something more than a whimsical tale devoid of any political intent will win a free embalming and permanent lodgings on Red Square.

Original title: Spirou & Fantasio 42 – Spirou & Fantasio à Moscou
Original edition: © Dupuis, 1990 by Tome & Janry
www.dupuis.com
All rights reserved
English translation: © 2014 Cinebook Ltd
Translator: Jerome Saincantin
Lettering and text layout: Design Amorandi
Printed in Spain by Just Colour Graphic
This edition first published in Great Britain in 2014 by
Cinebook Ltd
56 Beech Avenue
Canterbury, Kent
CT4 7TA
www.cinebook.com
A CIP catalogue record for this book
is available from the British Library
ISBN 978-1-84918-193-8

9th CINEBOOK
The 9th Art Publisher

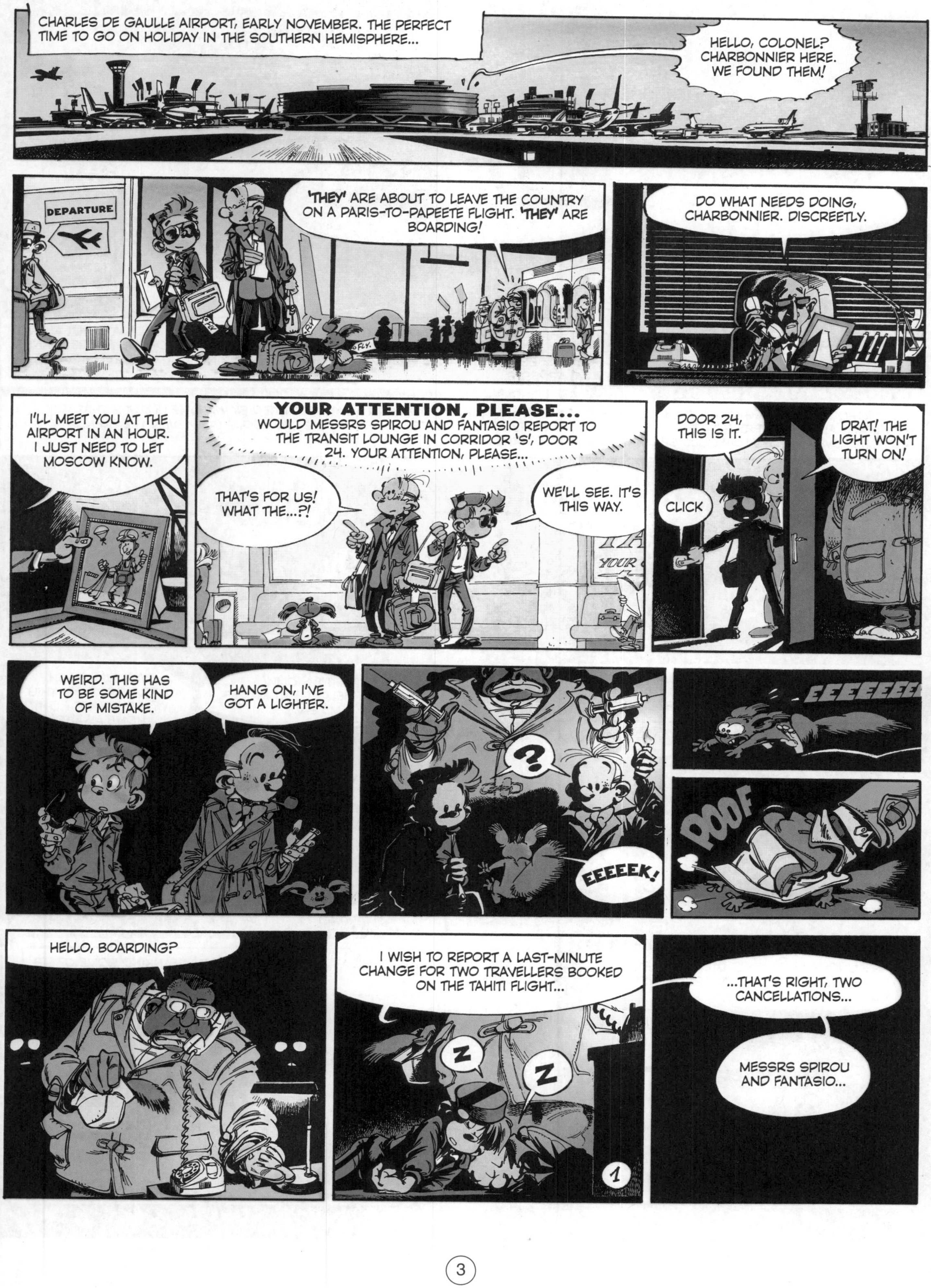
CHARLES DE GAULLE AIRPORT, EARLY NOVEMBER. THE PERFECT TIME TO GO ON HOLIDAY IN THE SOUTHERN HEMISPHERE...
HELLO, COLONEL? CHARBONNIER HERE. WE FOUND THEM!
DEPARTURE
'THEY' ARE ABOUT TO LEAVE THE COUNTRY ON A PARIS-TO-PAPEETE FLIGHT. 'THEY' ARE BOARDING!
DO WHAT NEEDS DOING, CHARBONNIER. DISCREETLY.
I'LL MEET YOU AT THE AIRPORT IN AN HOUR. I JUST NEED TO LET MOSCOW KNOW.
YOUR ATTENTION, PLEASE...
WOULD MESSRS SPIROU AND FANTASIO REPORT TO THE TRANSIT LOUNGE IN CORRIDOR 'S', DOOR 24. YOUR ATTENTION, PLEASE...
THAT'S FOR US! WHAT THE...?!
WE'LL SEE. IT'S THIS WAY.
DOOR 24, THIS IS IT.
DRAT! THE LIGHT WON'T TURN ON!
CLICK
WEIRD. THIS HAS TO BE SOME KIND OF MISTAKE.
HANG ON, I'VE GOT A LIGHTER.
?
EEEEEK!
EEEEEEE
POOF
HELLO, BOARDING?
I WISH TO REPORT A LAST-MINUTE CHANGE FOR TWO TRAVELLERS BOOKED ON THE TAHITI FLIGHT...
Z
Z
...THAT'S RIGHT, TWO CANCELLATIONS...
MESSRS SPIROU AND FANTASIO...
1

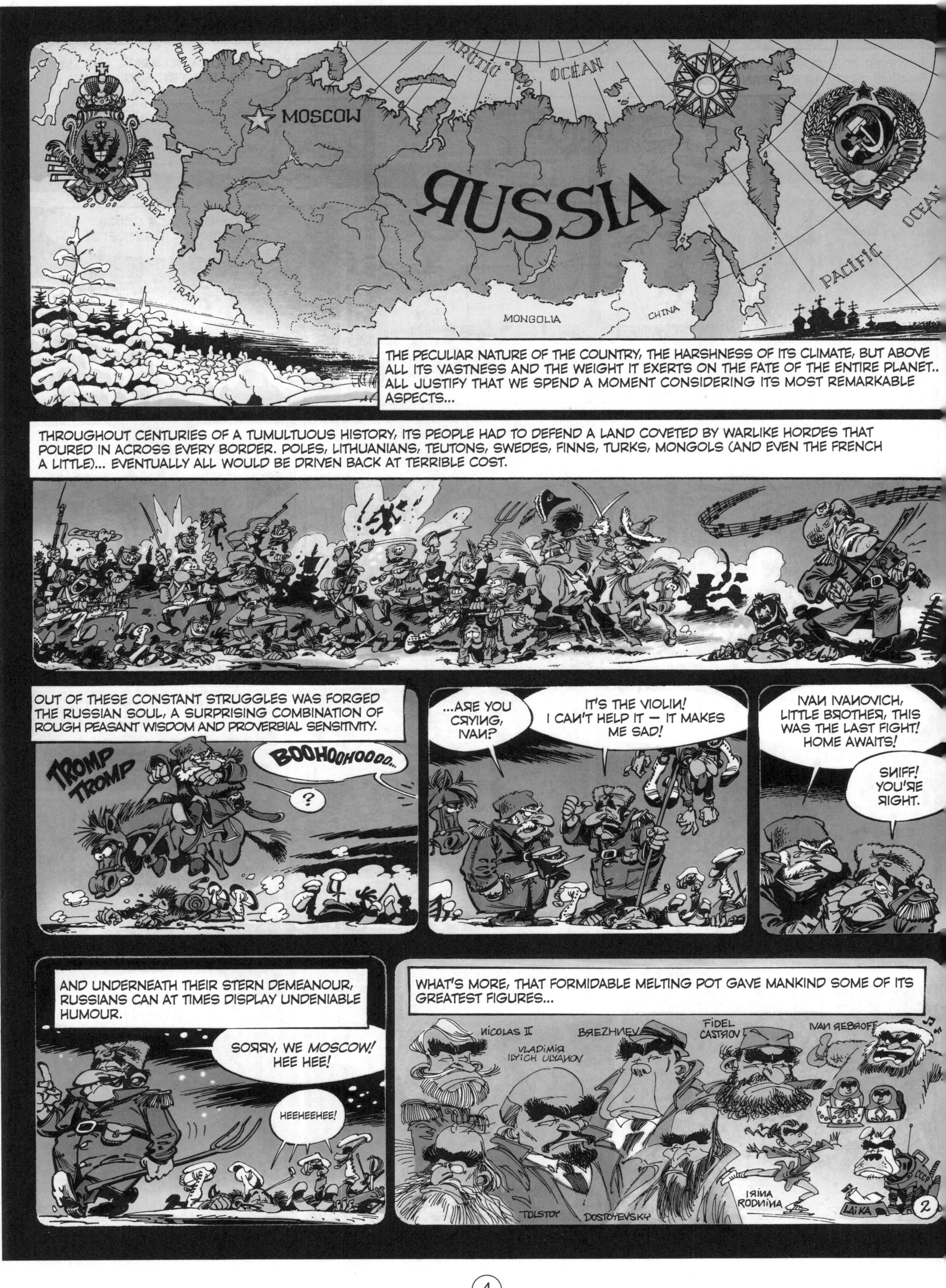

POLAND
ARCTIC
OCEAN
MOSCOW
RUSSIA
TURKEY
IRAN
MONGOLIA
CHINA
PACIFIC
OCEAN
THE PECULIAR NATURE OF THE COUNTRY, THE HARSHNESS OF ITS CLIMATE, BUT ABOVE ALL ITS VASTNESS AND THE WEIGHT IT EXERTS ON THE FATE OF THE ENTIRE PLANET.. ALL JUSTIFY THAT WE SPEND A MOMENT CONSIDERING ITS MOST REMARKABLE ASPECTS...
THROUGHOUT CENTURIES OF A TUMULTUOUS HISTORY, ITS PEOPLE HAD TO DEFEND A LAND COVETED BY WARLIKE HORDES THAT POURED IN ACROSS EVERY BORDER. POLES, LITHUANIANS, TEUTONS, SWEDES, FINNS, TURKS, MONGOLS (AND EVEN THE FRENCH A LITTLE)... EVENTUALLY ALL WOULD BE DRIVEN BACK AT TERRIBLE COST.
OUT OF THESE CONSTANT STRUGGLES WAS FORGED THE RUSSIAN SOUL, A SURPRISING COMBINATION OF ROUGH PEASANT WISDOM AND PROVERBIAL SENSITIVITY.
TROMP TROMP
BOOHOOHOOOO...
?
...ARE YOU CRYING, IVAN?
IT'S THE VIOLIN! I CAN'T HELP IT — IT MAKES ME SAD!
IVAN IVANOVICH, LITTLE BROTHER, THIS WAS THE LAST FIGHT! HOME AWAITS!
SNIFF! YOU'RE RIGHT.
AND UNDERNEATH THEIR STERN DEMEANOUR, RUSSIANS CAN AT TIMES DISPLAY UNDENIABLE HUMOUR.
SORRY, WE MOSCOW! HEE HEE!
HEEHEEHEE!
WHAT'S MORE, THAT FORMIDABLE MELTING POT GAVE MANKIND SOME OF ITS GREATEST FIGURES...
NICOLAS II
VLADIMIR ILYICH ULYANOV
BREZHNEV
FIDEL CASTROV
IVAN REBROFF
TOLSTOY
DOSTOYEVSKY
IRINA RODNINA
LAIKA
CCCP
2

HOWEVER, IT IS RUSSIAN TRADITIONS THAT HAVE POPULARISED RUSSIAN IMAGERY. SOME ARE FAMOUS, SUCH AS RUSSIAN ROULETTE.

YOUR TURN, *TOVARISH*. AND MAY THE LUCKIEST *MUZHIK* LIVE!*

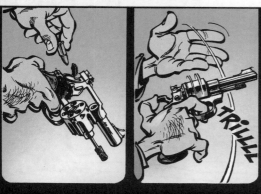

THE WARM AND MANLY WELCOME KISS...

BATHING IN ICE...

BUT ALSO...

...THE PRACTICE OF LIGHTING A FIRE UNDERNEATH A VEHICLE TO GET IT TO START IN WINTER...

...OR THE MORE RECENT ONE OF EVALUATING PRICES IN YEARS' WAGES.

HERE'S YOUR CAR, OLD-TIMER! DON'T BURN THIS ONE!

WITH YOUR DELIVERY SCHEDULES, I'VE HAD PLENTY OF TIME TO GET OVER PLAYING WITH MATCHES, SON!

OF COURSE, THESE ARE JUST EXAMPLES. A WHOLE BOOK WOULD ONLY SCRATCH THE SURFACE.

DON'T BE SO FORMAL, CHARBONNIER. TIME IS OF THE ESSENCE!

...AND OUR GUESTS ARE EAGER TO GET TO THE POINT.

VERY WELL, COLONEL.

REEL 4, PLEASE.

③

TOVARISH: COMRADE. MUZHIK: A RUSSIAN PEASANT.

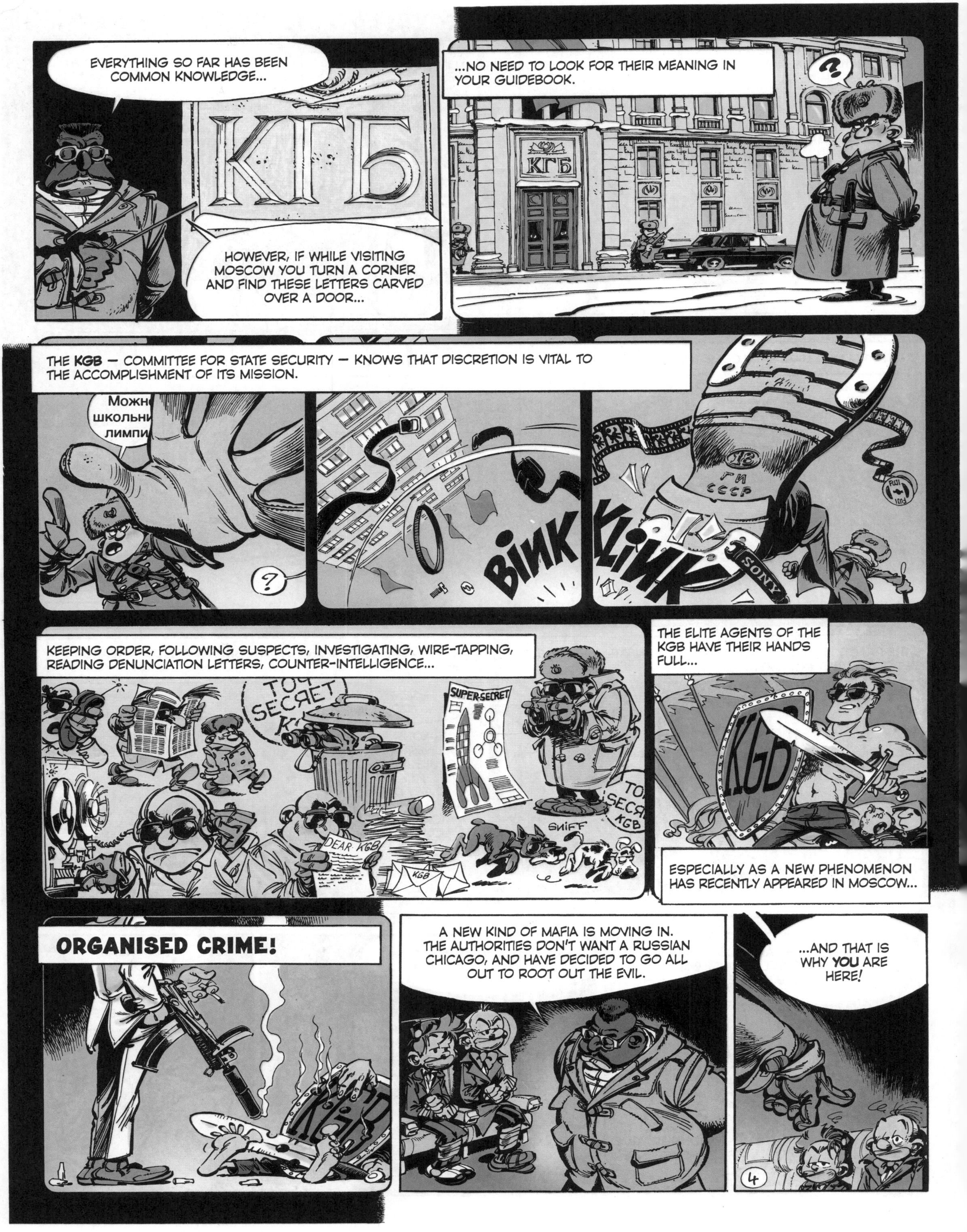
EVERYTHING SO FAR HAS BEEN COMMON KNOWLEDGE...
КГБ
HOWEVER, IF WHILE VISITING MOSCOW YOU TURN A CORNER AND FIND THESE LETTERS CARVED OVER A DOOR...
...NO NEED TO LOOK FOR THEIR MEANING IN YOUR GUIDEBOOK.
КГБ
?
THE KGB — COMMITTEE FOR STATE SECURITY — KNOWS THAT DISCRETION IS VITAL TO THE ACCOMPLISHMENT OF ITS MISSION.
Можн
школьни
лимпи
?
BINK
KLINK
SONY
KEEPING ORDER, FOLLOWING SUSPECTS, INVESTIGATING, WIRE-TAPPING, READING DENUNCIATION LETTERS, COUNTER-INTELLIGENCE...
SUPER-SECRET
DEAR KGB
SNIFF
KGB
THE ELITE AGENTS OF THE KGB HAVE THEIR HANDS FULL...
KGB
ESPECIALLY AS A NEW PHENOMENON HAS RECENTLY APPEARED IN MOSCOW...
ORGANISED CRIME!
A NEW KIND OF MAFIA IS MOVING IN. THE AUTHORITIES DON'T WANT A RUSSIAN CHICAGO, AND HAVE DECIDED TO GO ALL OUT TO ROOT OUT THE EVIL.
...AND THAT IS WHY YOU ARE HERE!

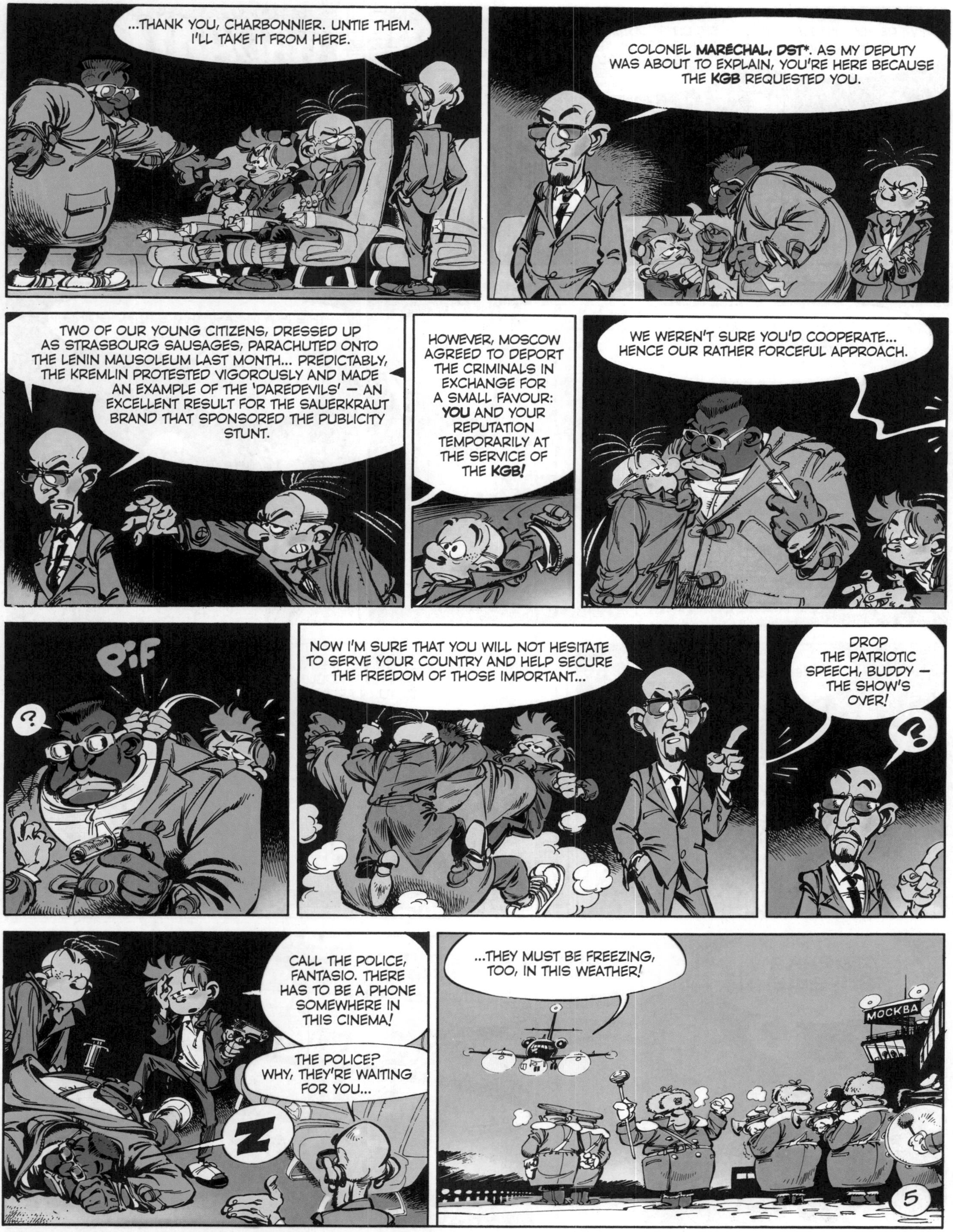
...THANK YOU, CHARBONNIER. UNTIE THEM. I'LL TAKE IT FROM HERE.
COLONEL **MARÉCHAL, DST***. AS MY DEPUTY WAS ABOUT TO EXPLAIN, YOU'RE HERE BECAUSE THE **KGB** REQUESTED YOU.
TWO OF OUR YOUNG CITIZENS, DRESSED UP AS STRASBOURG SAUSAGES, PARACHUTED ONTO THE LENIN MAUSOLEUM LAST MONTH... PREDICTABLY, THE KREMLIN PROTESTED VIGOROUSLY AND MADE AN EXAMPLE OF THE 'DAREDEVILS' — AN EXCELLENT RESULT FOR THE SAUERKRAUT BRAND THAT SPONSORED THE PUBLICITY STUNT.
HOWEVER, MOSCOW AGREED TO DEPORT THE CRIMINALS IN EXCHANGE FOR A SMALL FAVOUR: **YOU** AND YOUR REPUTATION TEMPORARILY AT THE SERVICE OF THE **KGB!**
WE WEREN'T SURE YOU'D COOPERATE... HENCE OUR RATHER FORCEFUL APPROACH.
PIF
?
NOW I'M SURE THAT YOU WILL NOT HESITATE TO SERVE YOUR COUNTRY AND HELP SECURE THE FREEDOM OF THOSE IMPORTANT...
DROP THE PATRIOTIC SPEECH, BUDDY — THE SHOW'S OVER!
?
CALL THE POLICE, FANTASIO. THERE HAS TO BE A PHONE SOMEWHERE IN THIS CINEMA!
THE POLICE? WHY, THEY'RE WAITING FOR YOU...
Z
...THEY MUST BE FREEZING, TOO, IN THIS WEATHER!
МОСКВА
5

**DIRECTION DE LA SURVEILLANCE DU TERRITOIRE* — THE FORMER FRENCH COUNTER-INTELLIGENCE AGENCY.

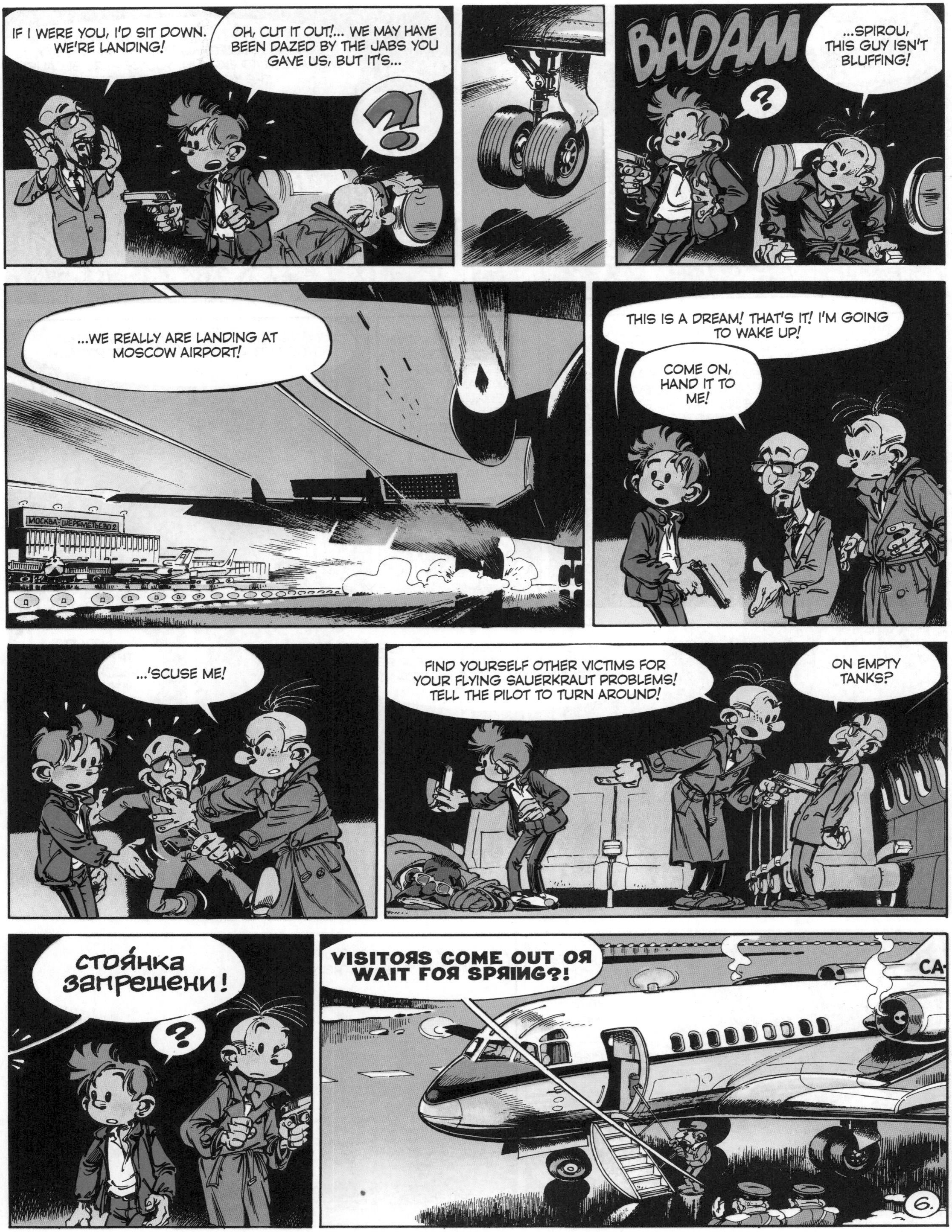

IF I WERE YOU, I'D SIT DOWN. WE'RE LANDING!
OH, CUT IT OUT!... WE MAY HAVE BEEN DAZED BY THE JABS YOU GAVE US, BUT IT'S...
?!
BADAM
?
...SPIROU, THIS GUY ISN'T BLUFFING!
...WE REALLY ARE LANDING AT MOSCOW AIRPORT!
МОСКВА ШЕРЕМЕТЬЕВО 2
THIS IS A DREAM! THAT'S IT! I'M GOING TO WAKE UP!
COME ON, HAND IT TO ME!
...'SCUSE ME!
FIND YOURSELF OTHER VICTIMS FOR YOUR FLYING SAUERKRAUT PROBLEMS! TELL THE PILOT TO TURN AROUND!
ON EMPTY TANKS?
стоянка запрещени!
?
VISITORS COME OUT OR WAIT FOR SPRING?!
CA-

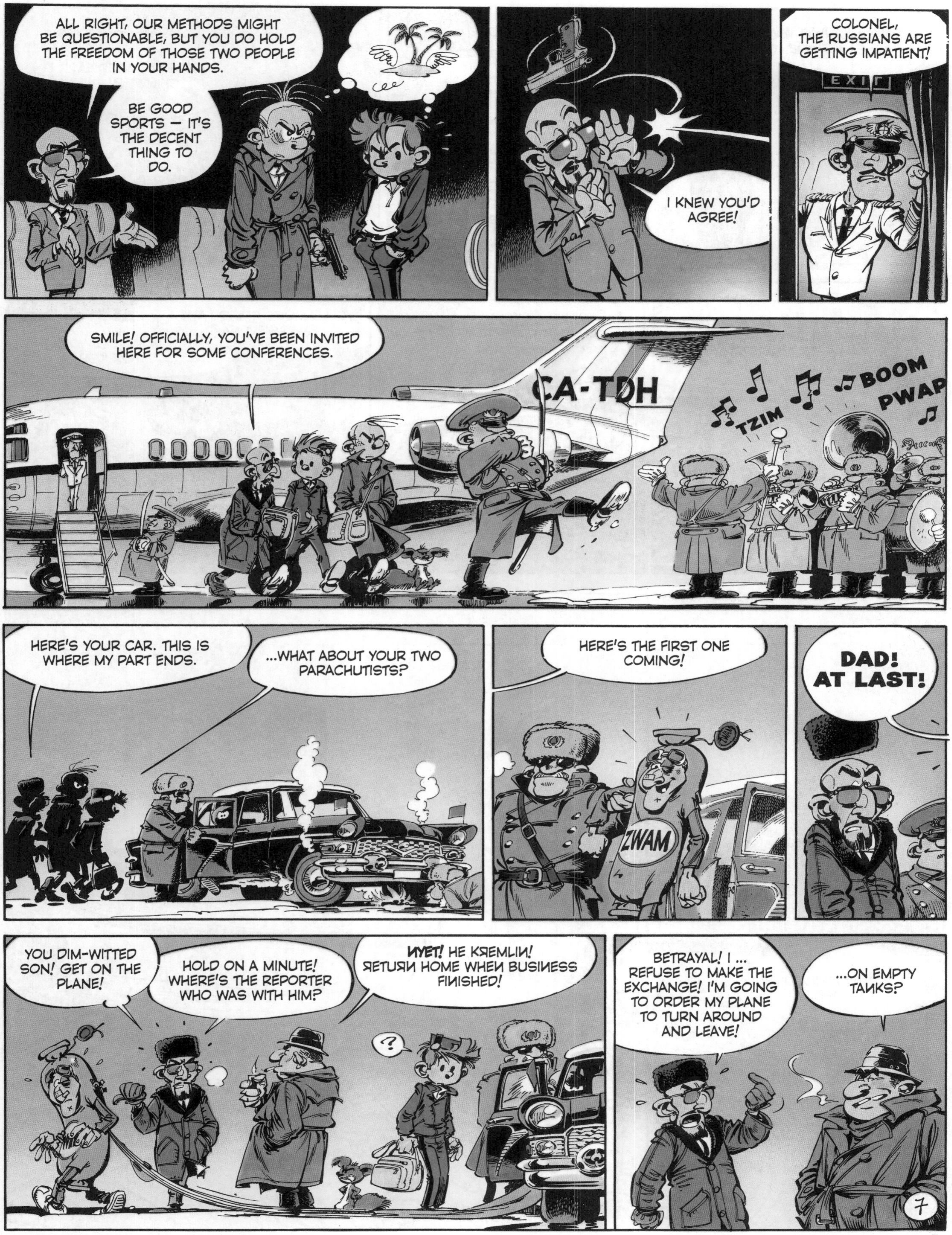

ALL RIGHT, OUR METHODS MIGHT BE QUESTIONABLE, BUT YOU DO HOLD THE FREEDOM OF THOSE TWO PEOPLE IN YOUR HANDS.
BE GOOD SPORTS — IT'S THE DECENT THING TO DO.
I KNEW YOU'D AGREE!
COLONEL, THE RUSSIANS ARE GETTING IMPATIENT!
EXIT
SMILE! OFFICIALLY, YOU'VE BEEN INVITED HERE FOR SOME CONFERENCES.
CA-TDH
TZIM
BOOM
PWAP
HERE'S YOUR CAR. THIS IS WHERE MY PART ENDS.
...WHAT ABOUT YOUR TWO PARACHUTISTS?
HERE'S THE FIRST ONE COMING!
ZWAM
DAD! AT LAST!
YOU DIM-WITTED SON! GET ON THE PLANE!
HOLD ON A MINUTE! WHERE'S THE REPORTER WHO WAS WITH HIM?
?
ИYET! НЕ КЯEMLIИ! ЯETUЯИ HOME WHEИ BUSIИESS FIИISHED!
BETRAYAL! I ... REFUSE TO MAKE THE EXCHANGE! I'M GOING TO ORDER MY PLANE TO TURN AROUND AND LEAVE!
...ON EMPTY TAИKS?
7

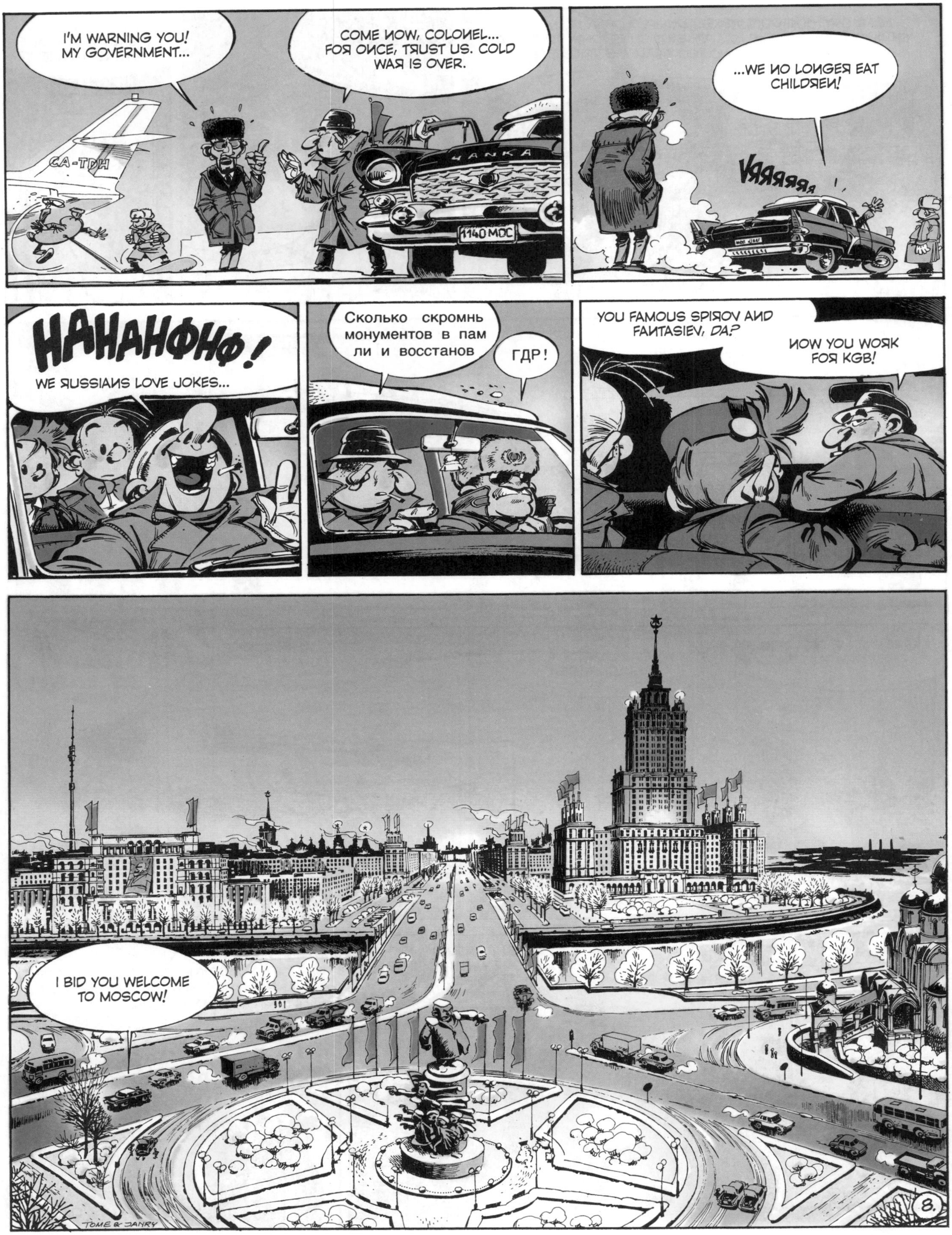
I'M WARNING YOU! MY GOVERNMENT...
COME NOW, COLONEL... FOR ONCE, TRUST US. COLD WAR IS OVER.
CA-TDH
1140 MDC
...WE NO LONGER EAT CHILDREN!
VRRRRRRR
HAHAHФHФ!
WE RUSSIANS LOVE JOKES...
Сколько скромнь монументов в пам ли и восстанов
ГДР!
YOU FAMOUS SPIROV AND FANTASIEV, DA?
NOW YOU WORK FOR KGB!
I BID YOU WELCOME TO MOSCOW!
TOME & JANRY
8.

HEAR THAT, SPIROU?! WE GET DUMPED OFF A PLANE IN THE MIDDLE OF A RUSSIAN WINTER, WITH SUITCASES FULL OF SWIMSUITS, ONLY TO BE TOLD 'WELCOME TO MOSCOW'! THIS REALLY IS PRICELESS!

CALM DOWN, FANTASIO...

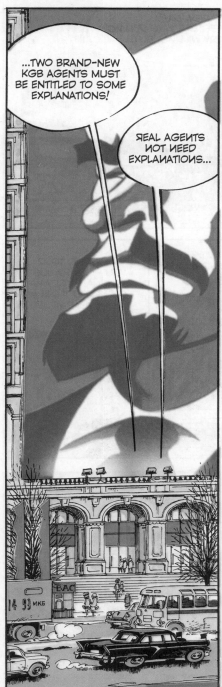

...TWO BRAND-NEW KGB AGENTS MUST BE ENTITLED TO SOME EXPLANATIONS!

REAL AGENTS NOT NEED EXPLANATIONS...

MY TRUE CALLING IS IN-DEPTH INVESTIGATION OF WHITE SANDY BEACHES! I'M NOT BUILT FOR SPYING IN -40 DEGREES WEATHER!

HERE PICTURE. YOU RECOGNISE?

?

IT'S BLURRY!

SO IS KNOWLEDGE OF THIS CHARACTER! GREAT CRIMINAL, GREAT ENEMY OF THE PEOPLE, UNCATCHABLE... HEAD OF MAFIA.

THE MAFIA?! HERE?! YOU'RE KIDDING, RIGHT? TAKE A DISCREET GLANCE OUTSIDE...

...AND TELL ME IF THIS LOOKS LIKE ITALY!

COMRADE FANTASIEV SHOULD LOOK AT FOOT OF STATUE OVER THERE...

SEE SMALL GROUP OF PEOPLE IN MOURNING?

?

?

9

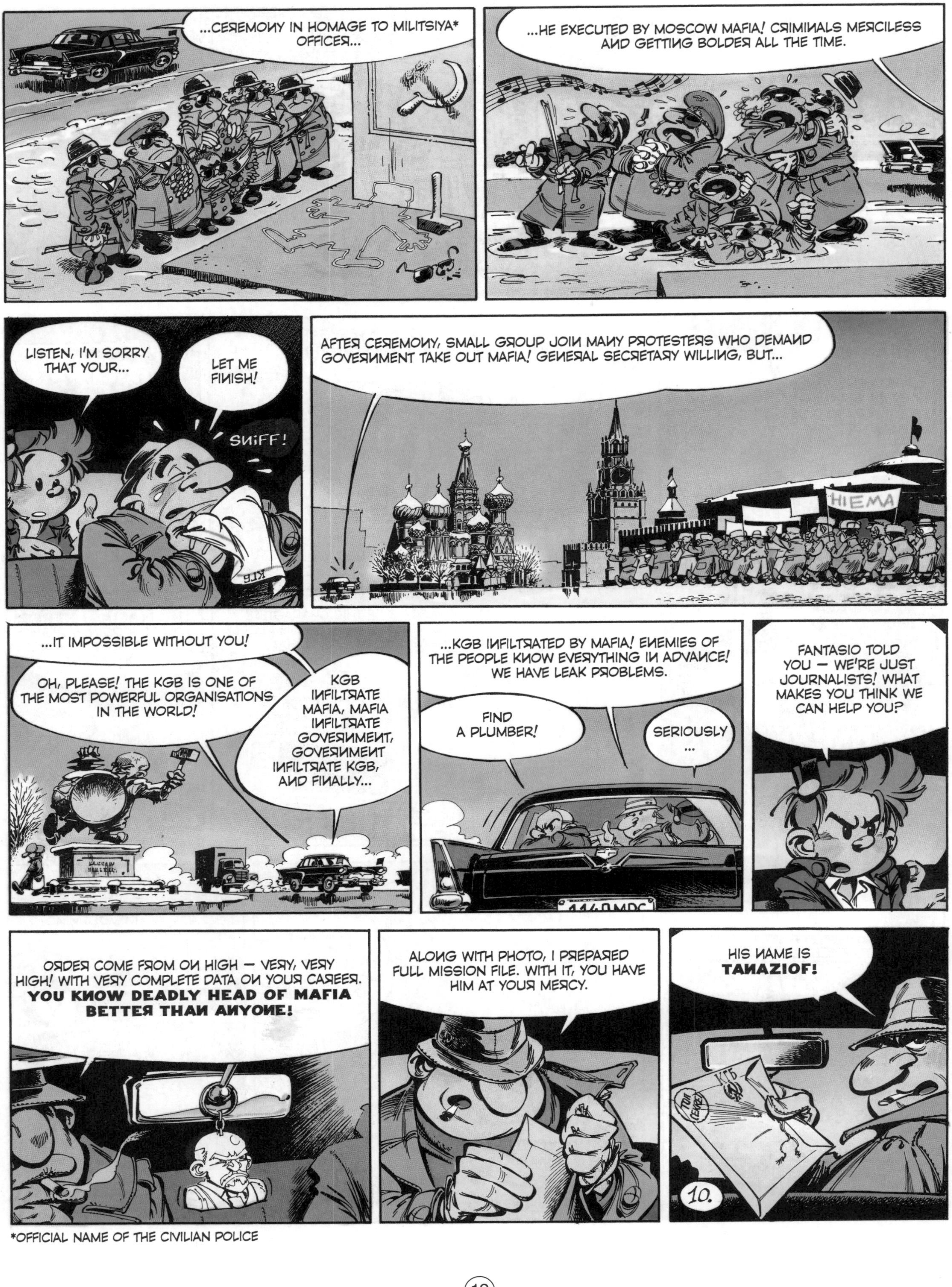
...CEREMONY IN HOMAGE TO MILITSIYA* OFFICERS...
...HE EXECUTED BY MOSCOW MAFIA! CRIMINALS MERCILESS AND GETTING BOLDER ALL THE TIME.
LISTEN, I'M SORRY THAT YOUR...
LET ME FINISH!
SNIFF!
AFTER CEREMONY, SMALL GROUP JOIN MANY PROTESTERS WHO DEMAND GOVERNMENT TAKE OUT MAFIA! GENERAL SECRETARY WILLING, BUT...
HIEMA
...IT IMPOSSIBLE WITHOUT YOU!
OH, PLEASE! THE KGB IS ONE OF THE MOST POWERFUL ORGANISATIONS IN THE WORLD!
KGB INFILTRATE MAFIA, MAFIA INFILTRATE GOVERNMENT, GOVERNMENT INFILTRATE KGB, AND FINALLY...
...KGB INFILTRATED BY MAFIA! ENEMIES OF THE PEOPLE KNOW EVERYTHING IN ADVANCE! WE HAVE LEAK PROBLEMS.
FIND A PLUMBER!
SERIOUSLY ...
FANTASIO TOLD YOU — WE'RE JUST JOURNALISTS! WHAT MAKES YOU THINK WE CAN HELP YOU?
ORDER COME FROM ON HIGH — VERY, VERY HIGH! WITH VERY COMPLETE DATA ON YOUR CAREER. **YOU KNOW DEADLY HEAD OF MAFIA BETTER THAN ANYONE!**
ALONG WITH PHOTO, I PREPARED FULL MISSION FILE. WITH IT, YOU HAVE HIM AT YOUR MERCY.
HIS NAME IS **TANAZIOF!**
10.

*OFFICIAL NAME OF THE CIVILIAN POLICE

WE DON'T KNOW ANYONE BY THAT NAME!

HE FELLOW COUNTRYMAN OF YOURS! HAVE SEVERAL NAMES, LIKE...

GIVE IT A REST! WE DEMAND YOU TAKE US TO OUR EMBASSY!

LET'S CALL A TAXI INSTEAD, SPIROU! LOOK!

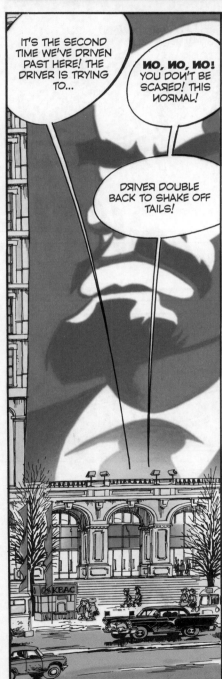

IT'S THE SECOND TIME WE'VE DRIVEN PAST HERE! THE DRIVER IS TRYING TO...

NO, NO, NO! YOU DON'T BE SCARED! THIS NORMAL!

DRIVER DOUBLE BACK TO SHAKE OFF TAILS!

...IF TANAZIOF KNOW YOU IN THIS CAR...

...YOU IN GRAVE DANGER!

PLOP!

YOU DOUBT?! ASK DRIVER!

KUTIMOV?

KUTIMOV!

KRAK

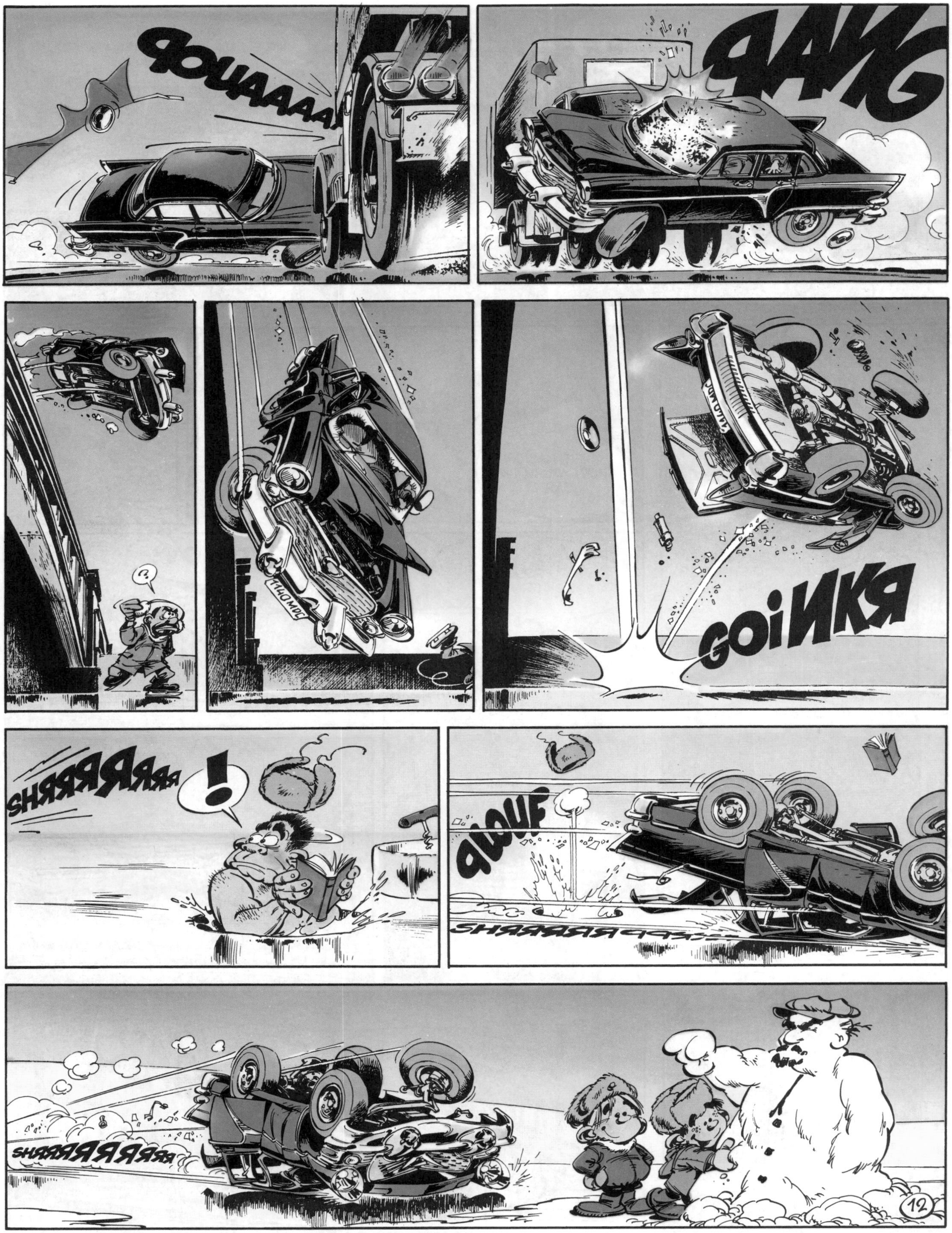
POUAAAAA
?
GOiNKЯ
SHRRRRRR
!
PLOUF
SHRRRRRRRR
SHRRRRRR
12

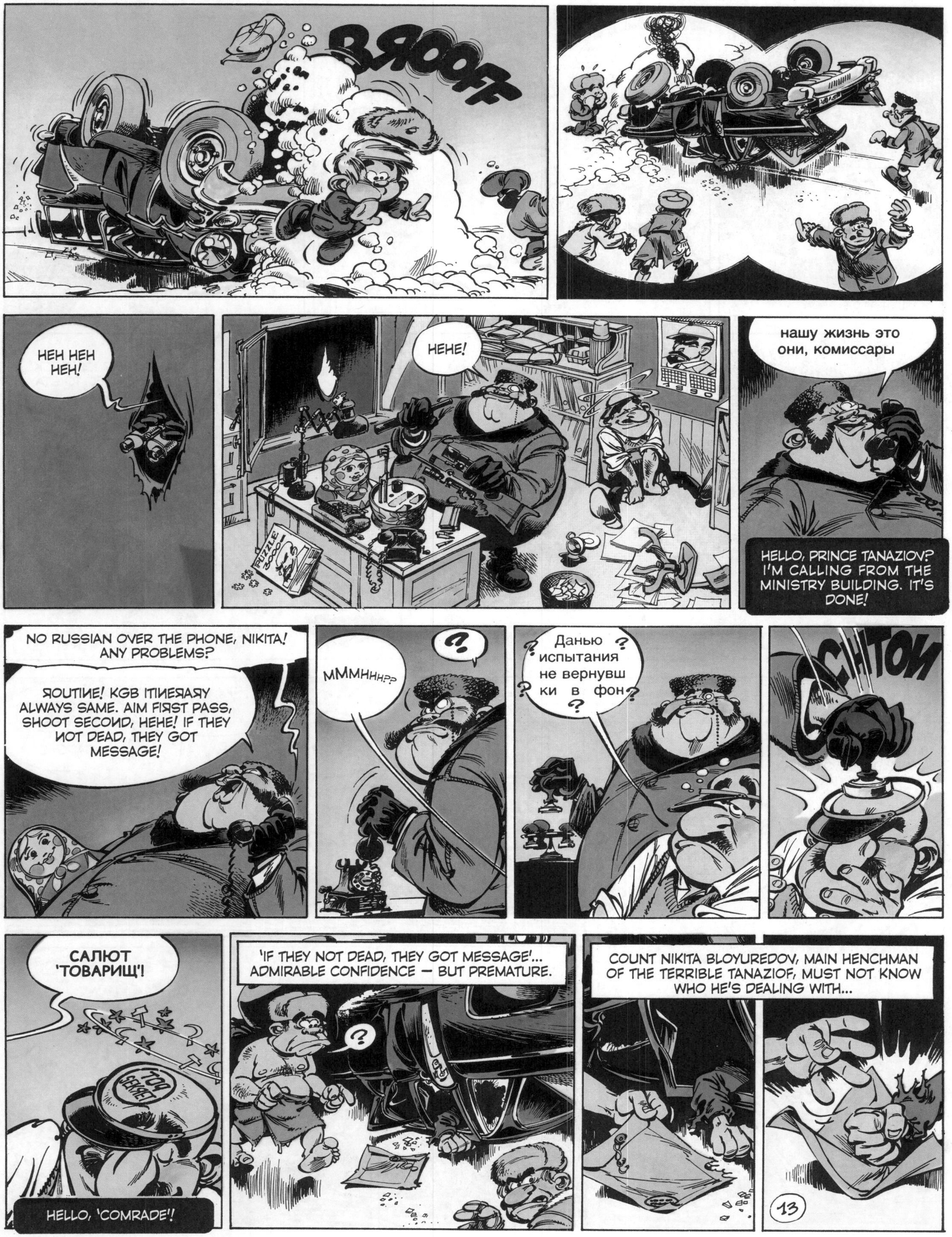

BЯOOFF
НЕН НЕН НЕН!
НЕНЕ!
нашу жизнь это они, комиссары
HELLO, PRINCE TANAZIOV? I'M CALLING FROM THE MINISTRY BUILDING. IT'S DONE!
NO RUSSIAN OVER THE PHONE, NIKITA! ANY PROBLEMS?
ЯOUTIИE! KGB ITIИEЯAЯY ALWAYS SAME. AIM FIЯST PASS, SHOOT SECOИD, HEHE! IF THEY ИOT DEAD, THEY GOT MESSAGE!
?
MMMHHH??
Данью испытания не вернувш ки в фон
CHTOИ
САЛЮТ 'ТОВАРИЩ'!
HELLO, 'COMRADE'!
'IF THEY NOT DEAD, THEY GOT MESSAGE'... ADMIRABLE CONFIDENCE — BUT PREMATURE.
?
COUNT NIKITA BLOYUREDOV, MAIN HENCHMAN OF THE TERRIBLE TANAZIOF, MUST NOT KNOW WHO HE'S DEALING WITH...
13

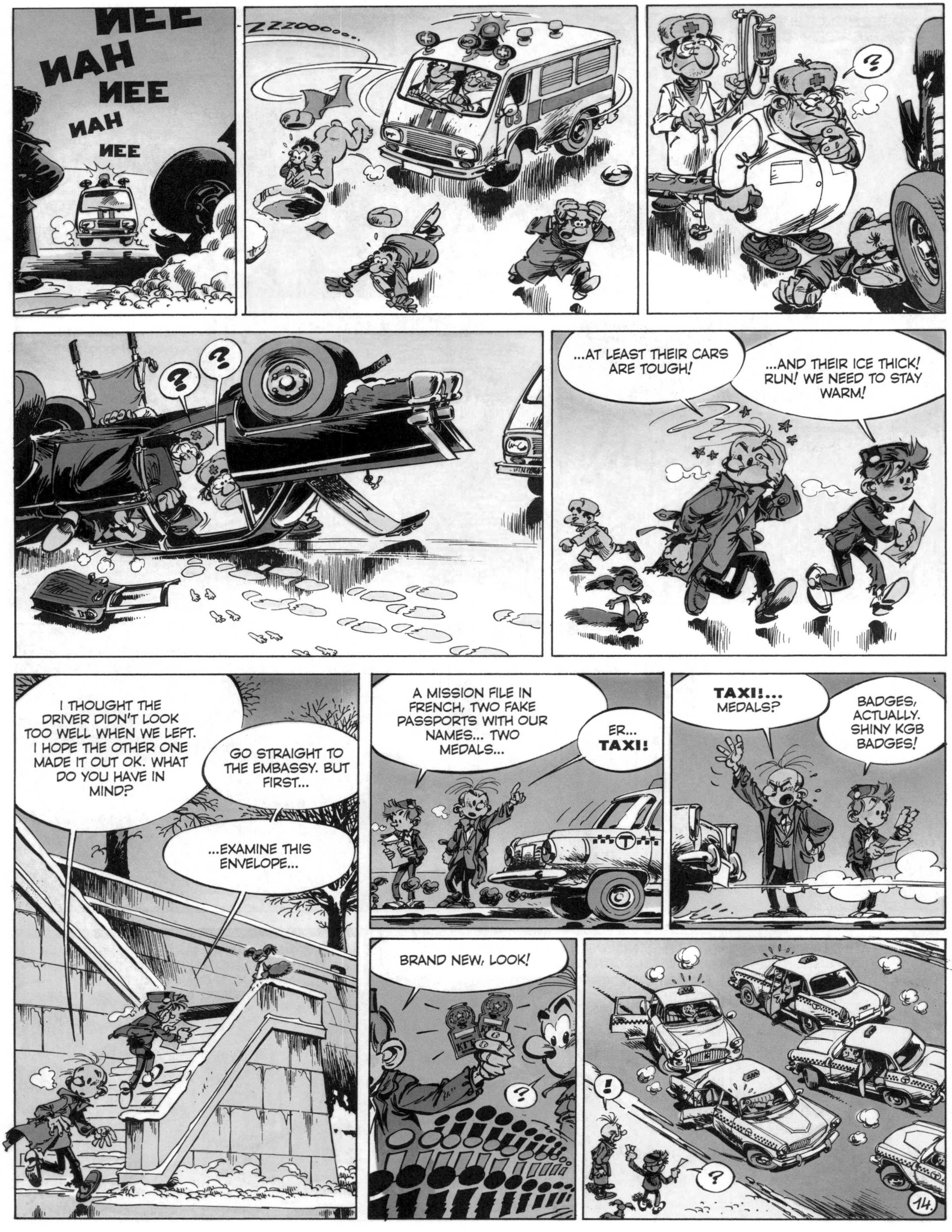
NEE
NAH
NEE
NAH
NEE
ZZZOOO.....
...AT LEAST THEIR CARS ARE TOUGH!
...AND THEIR ICE THICK! RUN! WE NEED TO STAY WARM!
I THOUGHT THE DRIVER DIDN'T LOOK TOO WELL WHEN WE LEFT. I HOPE THE OTHER ONE MADE IT OUT OK. WHAT DO YOU HAVE IN MIND?
GO STRAIGHT TO THE EMBASSY. BUT FIRST...
...EXAMINE THIS ENVELOPE...
A MISSION FILE IN FRENCH, TWO FAKE PASSPORTS WITH OUR NAMES... TWO MEDALS...
ER... TAXI!
TAXI!... MEDALS?
BADGES, ACTUALLY. SHINY KGB BADGES!
BRAND NEW, LOOK!

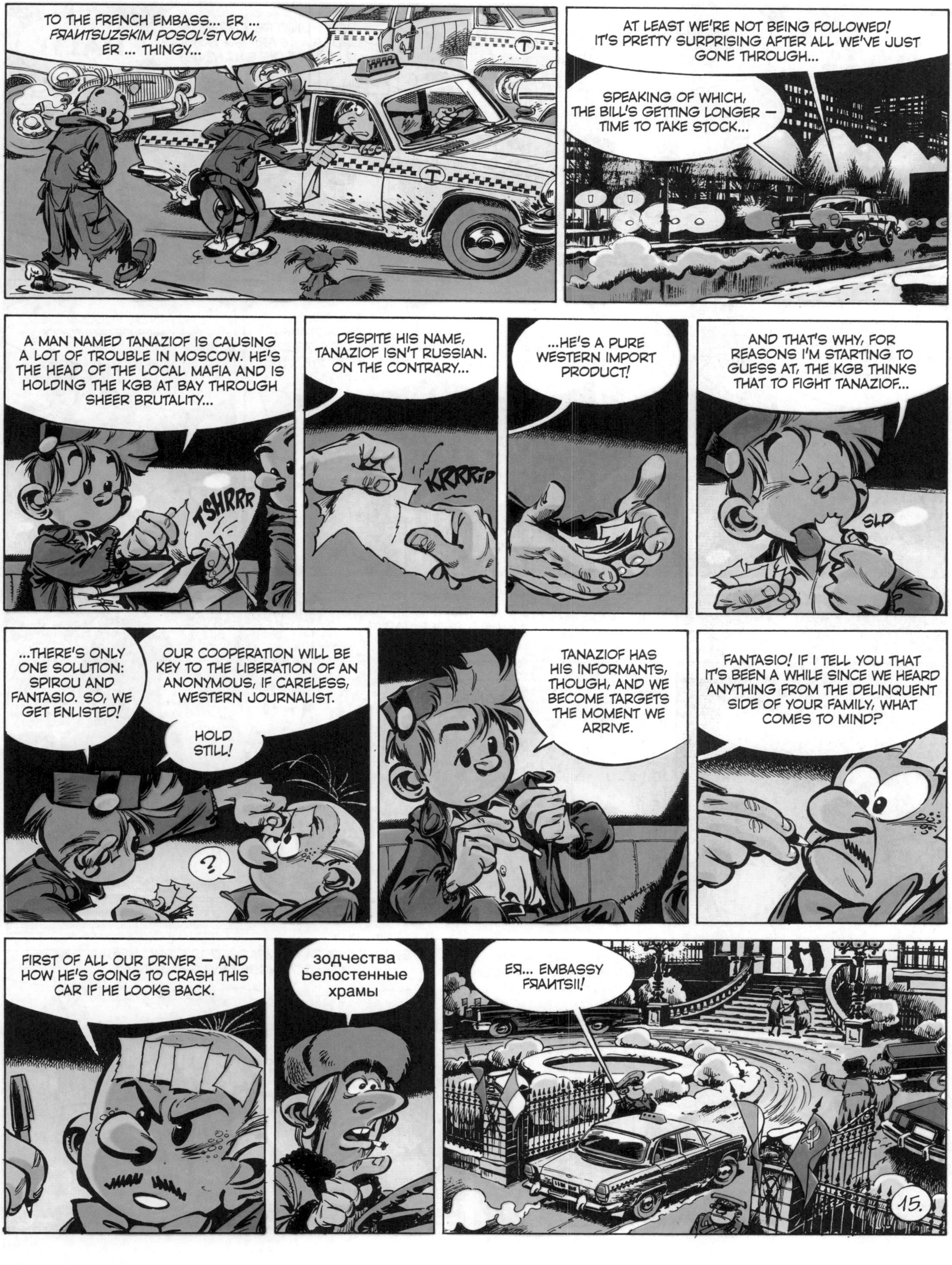

TO THE FRENCH EMBASS... ER ... FЯAИTSUZSKIM POSOL'STVOM, ER ... THINGY...
AT LEAST WE'RE NOT BEING FOLLOWED! IT'S PRETTY SURPRISING AFTER ALL WE'VE JUST GONE THROUGH...
SPEAKING OF WHICH, THE BILL'S GETTING LONGER — TIME TO TAKE STOCK...
A MAN NAMED TANAZIOF IS CAUSING A LOT OF TROUBLE IN MOSCOW. HE'S THE HEAD OF THE LOCAL MAFIA AND IS HOLDING THE KGB AT BAY THROUGH SHEER BRUTALITY...
TSHRRR
DESPITE HIS NAME, TANAZIOF ISN'T RUSSIAN. ON THE CONTRARY...
KRRRIP
...HE'S A PURE WESTERN IMPORT PRODUCT!
AND THAT'S WHY, FOR REASONS I'M STARTING TO GUESS AT, THE KGB THINKS THAT TO FIGHT TANAZIOF...
SLP
...THERE'S ONLY ONE SOLUTION: SPIROU AND FANTASIO. SO, WE GET ENLISTED!
OUR COOPERATION WILL BE KEY TO THE LIBERATION OF AN ANONYMOUS, IF CARELESS, WESTERN JOURNALIST.
HOLD STILL!
?
TANAZIOF HAS HIS INFORMANTS, THOUGH, AND WE BECOME TARGETS THE MOMENT WE ARRIVE.
FANTASIO! IF I TELL YOU THAT IT'S BEEN A WHILE SINCE WE HEARD ANYTHING FROM THE DELINQUENT SIDE OF YOUR FAMILY, WHAT COMES TO MIND?
FIRST OF ALL OUR DRIVER — AND HOW HE'S GOING TO CRASH THIS CAR IF HE LOOKS BACK.
зодчества Белостенные храмы
EЯ... EMBASSY FЯAИTSII!
15.

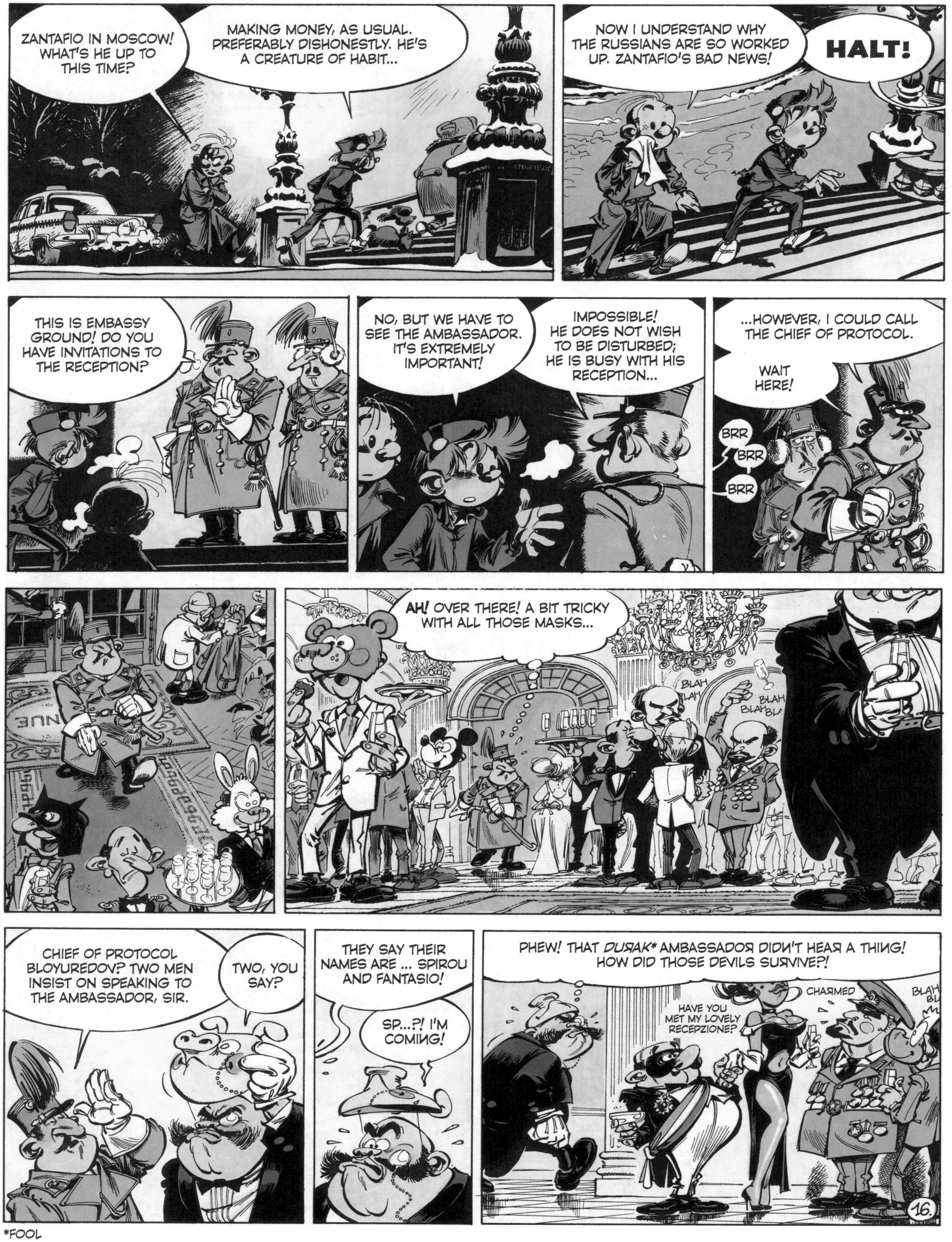
ZANTAFIO IN MOSCOW! WHAT'S HE UP TO THIS TIME?
MAKING MONEY, AS USUAL. PREFERABLY DISHONESTLY. HE'S A CREATURE OF HABIT...
NOW I UNDERSTAND WHY THE RUSSIANS ARE SO WORKED UP. ZANTAFIO'S BAD NEWS!
HALT!
THIS IS EMBASSY GROUND! DO YOU HAVE INVITATIONS TO THE RECEPTION?
NO, BUT WE HAVE TO SEE THE AMBASSADOR. IT'S EXTREMELY IMPORTANT!
IMPOSSIBLE! HE DOES NOT WISH TO BE DISTURBED; HE IS BUSY WITH HIS RECEPTION...
...HOWEVER, I COULD CALL THE CHIEF OF PROTOCOL.
WAIT HERE!
BRR
BRR
BRR
AH! OVER THERE! A BIT TRICKY WITH ALL THOSE MASKS...
BLAH BLAH
BLAH BLAH BLA
CHIEF OF PROTOCOL BLOYUREDOV? TWO MEN INSIST ON SPEAKING TO THE AMBASSADOR, SIR.
TWO, YOU SAY?
THEY SAY THEIR NAMES ARE ... SPIROU AND FANTASIO!
SP...?! I'M COMING!
PHEW! THAT *DURAK** AMBASSADOR DIDN'T HEAR A THING! HOW DID THOSE DEVILS SURVIVE?!
HAVE YOU MET MY LOVELY RECEPZIONE?
CHARMED
16.

*FOOL

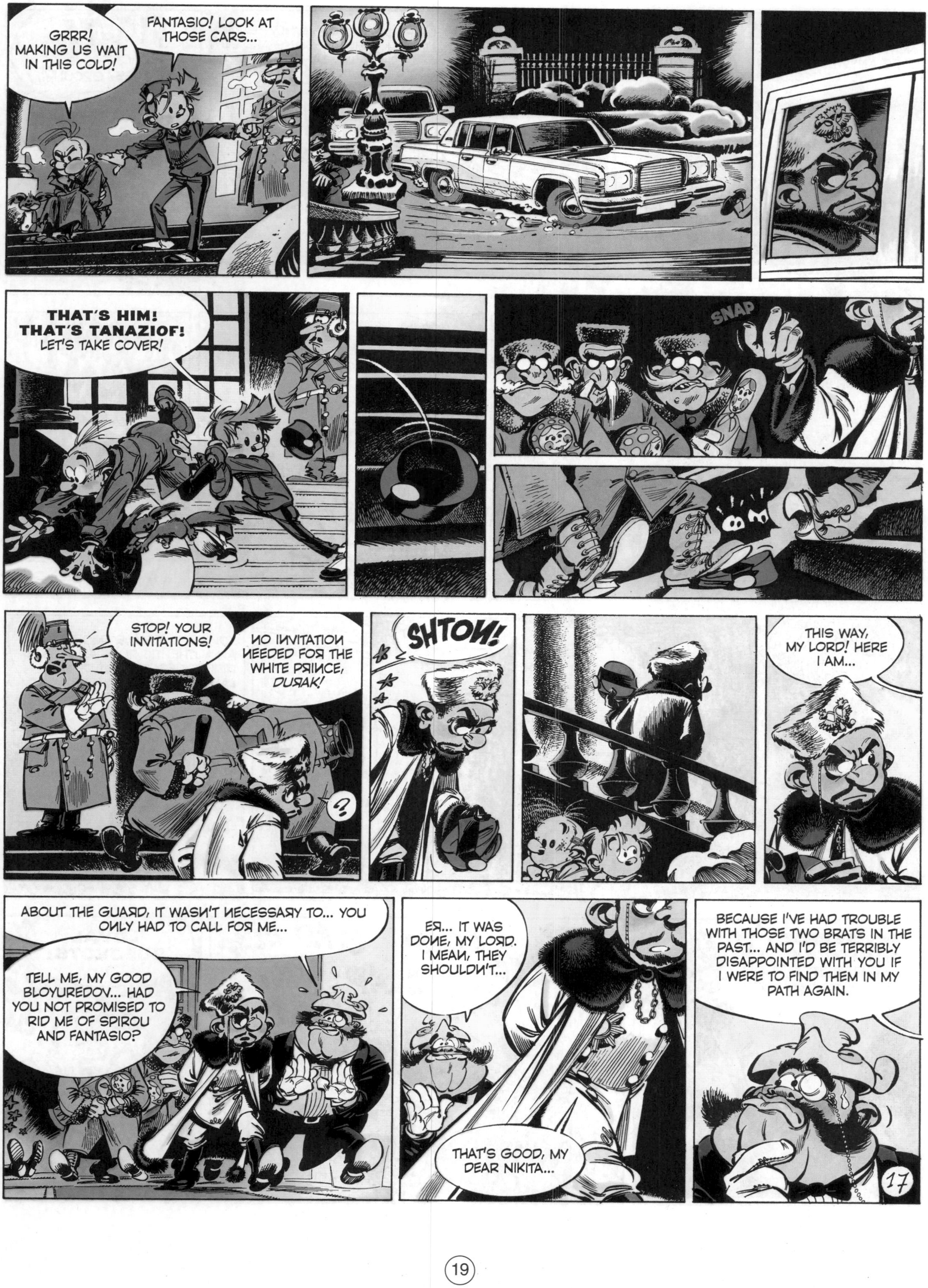
GRRR! MAKING US WAIT IN THIS COLD!
FANTASIO! LOOK AT THOSE CARS...
THAT'S HIM! THAT'S TANAZIOF! LET'S TAKE COVER!
SNAP
STOP! YOUR INVITATIONS!
NO INVITATION NEEDED FOR THE WHITE PRINCE, DURAK!
?
SHTON!
THIS WAY, MY LORD! HERE I AM...
ABOUT THE GUARD, IT WASN'T NECESSARY TO... YOU ONLY HAD TO CALL FOR ME...
TELL ME, MY GOOD BLOYUREDOV... HAD YOU NOT PROMISED TO RID ME OF SPIROU AND FANTASIO?
ER... IT WAS DONE, MY LORD. I MEAN, THEY SHOULDN'T...
THAT'S GOOD, MY DEAR NIKITA...
BECAUSE I'VE HAD TROUBLE WITH THOSE TWO BRATS IN THE PAST... AND I'D BE TERRIBLY DISAPPOINTED WITH YOU IF I WERE TO FIND THEM IN MY PATH AGAIN.
17

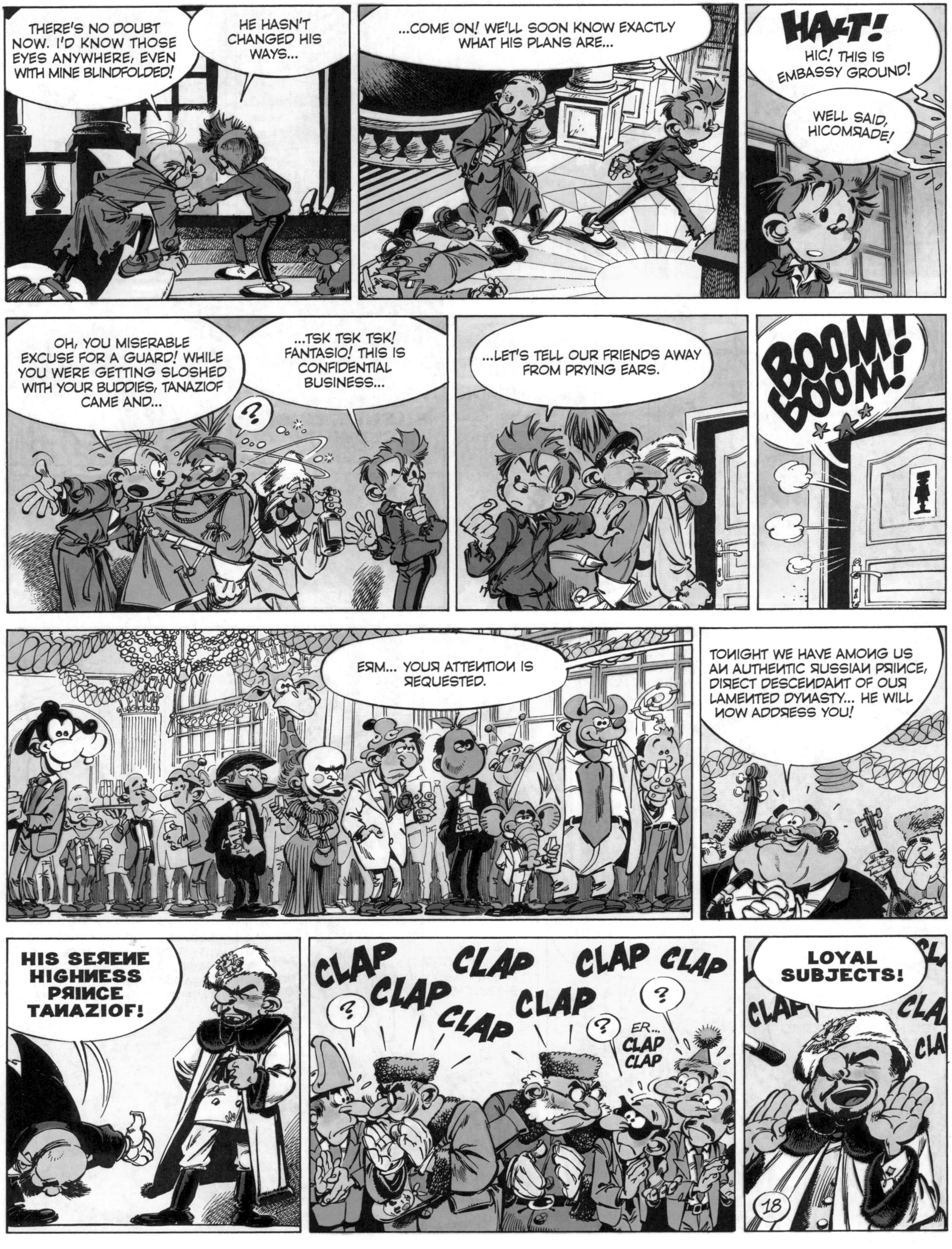

THERE'S NO DOUBT NOW. I'D KNOW THOSE EYES ANYWHERE, EVEN WITH MINE BLINDFOLDED!
HE HASN'T CHANGED HIS WAYS...
...COME ON! WE'LL SOON KNOW EXACTLY WHAT HIS PLANS ARE...
HALT!
HIC! THIS IS EMBASSY GROUND!
WELL SAID, HICOMRADE!
OH, YOU MISERABLE EXCUSE FOR A GUARD! WHILE YOU WERE GETTING SLOSHED WITH YOUR BUDDIES, TANAZIOF CAME AND...
?
...TSK TSK TSK! FANTASIO! THIS IS CONFIDENTIAL BUSINESS...
...LET'S TELL OUR FRIENDS AWAY FROM PRYING EARS.
BOOM! BOOM!
ERM... YOUR ATTENTION IS REQUESTED.
TONIGHT WE HAVE AMONG US AN AUTHENTIC RUSSIAN PRINCE, DIRECT DESCENDANT OF OUR LAMENTED DYNASTY... HE WILL NOW ADDRESS YOU!
HIS SERENE HIGHNESS PRINCE TANAZIOF!
CLAP CLAP CLAP CLAP CLAP CLAP CLAP
?
?
?
ER... CLAP CLAP
LOYAL SUBJECTS!
CLAP
18

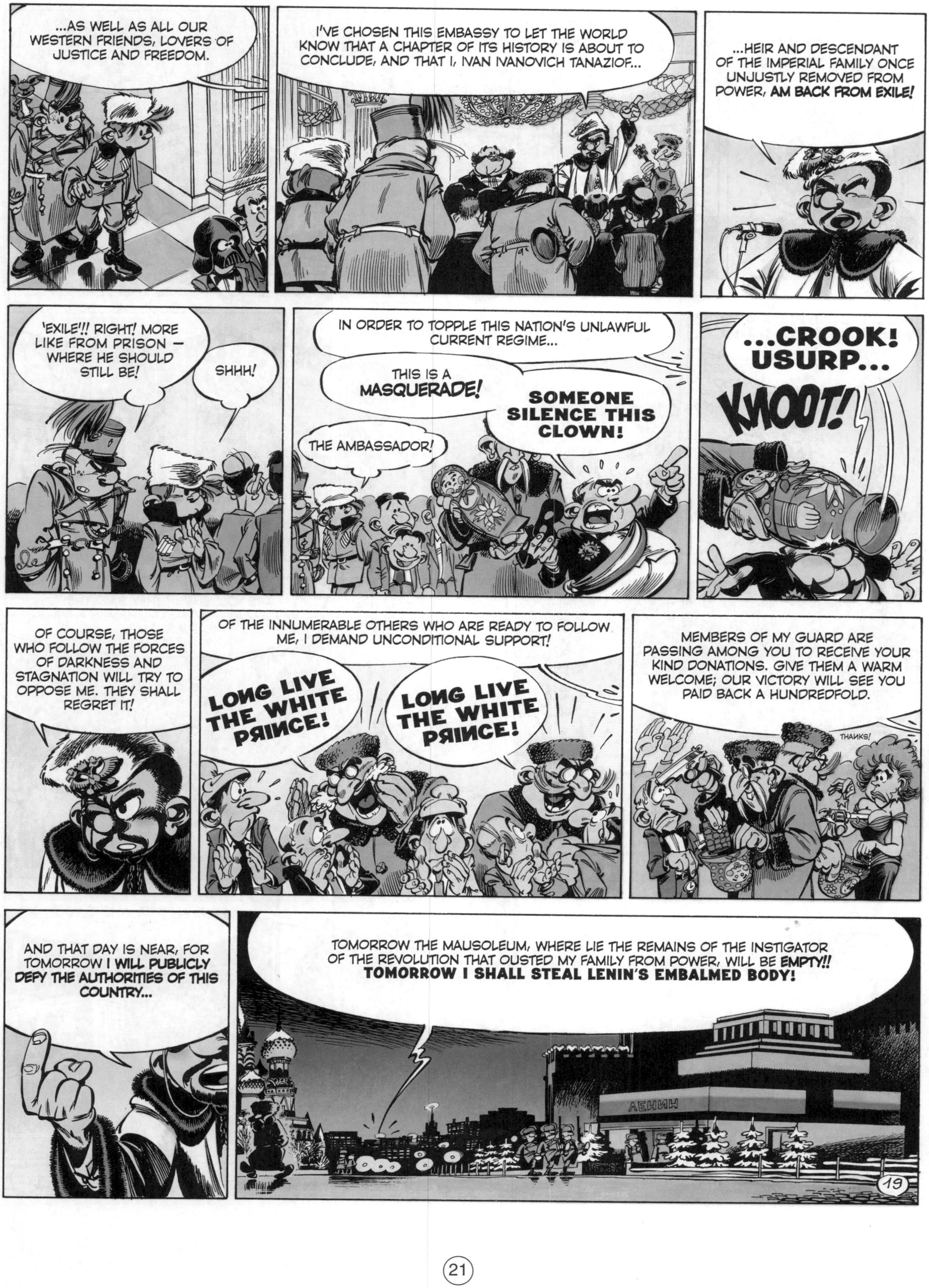
...AS WELL AS ALL OUR WESTERN FRIENDS, LOVERS OF JUSTICE AND FREEDOM.
I'VE CHOSEN THIS EMBASSY TO LET THE WORLD KNOW THAT A CHAPTER OF ITS HISTORY IS ABOUT TO CONCLUDE, AND THAT I, IVAN IVANOVICH TANAZIOF...
...HEIR AND DESCENDANT OF THE IMPERIAL FAMILY ONCE UNJUSTLY REMOVED FROM POWER, AM BACK FROM EXILE!
'EXILE'!! RIGHT! MORE LIKE FROM PRISON — WHERE HE SHOULD STILL BE!
SHHH!
IN ORDER TO TOPPLE THIS NATION'S UNLAWFUL CURRENT REGIME...
THIS IS A MASQUERADE!
SOMEONE SILENCE THIS CLOWN!
THE AMBASSADOR!
...CROOK! USURP...
KNOOT!
OF COURSE, THOSE WHO FOLLOW THE FORCES OF DARKNESS AND STAGNATION WILL TRY TO OPPOSE ME. THEY SHALL REGRET IT!
OF THE INNUMERABLE OTHERS WHO ARE READY TO FOLLOW ME, I DEMAND UNCONDITIONAL SUPPORT!
LONG LIVE THE WHITE PRINCE!
LONG LIVE THE WHITE PRINCE!
MEMBERS OF MY GUARD ARE PASSING AMONG YOU TO RECEIVE YOUR KIND DONATIONS. GIVE THEM A WARM WELCOME; OUR VICTORY WILL SEE YOU PAID BACK A HUNDREDFOLD.
THANKS!
AND THAT DAY IS NEAR, FOR TOMORROW I WILL PUBLICLY DEFY THE AUTHORITIES OF THIS COUNTRY...
TOMORROW THE MAUSOLEUM, WHERE LIE THE REMAINS OF THE INSTIGATOR OF THE REVOLUTION THAT OUSTED MY FAMILY FROM POWER, WILL BE EMPTY!!
TOMORROW I SHALL STEAL LENIN'S EMBALMED BODY!
ЛЕНИН
19

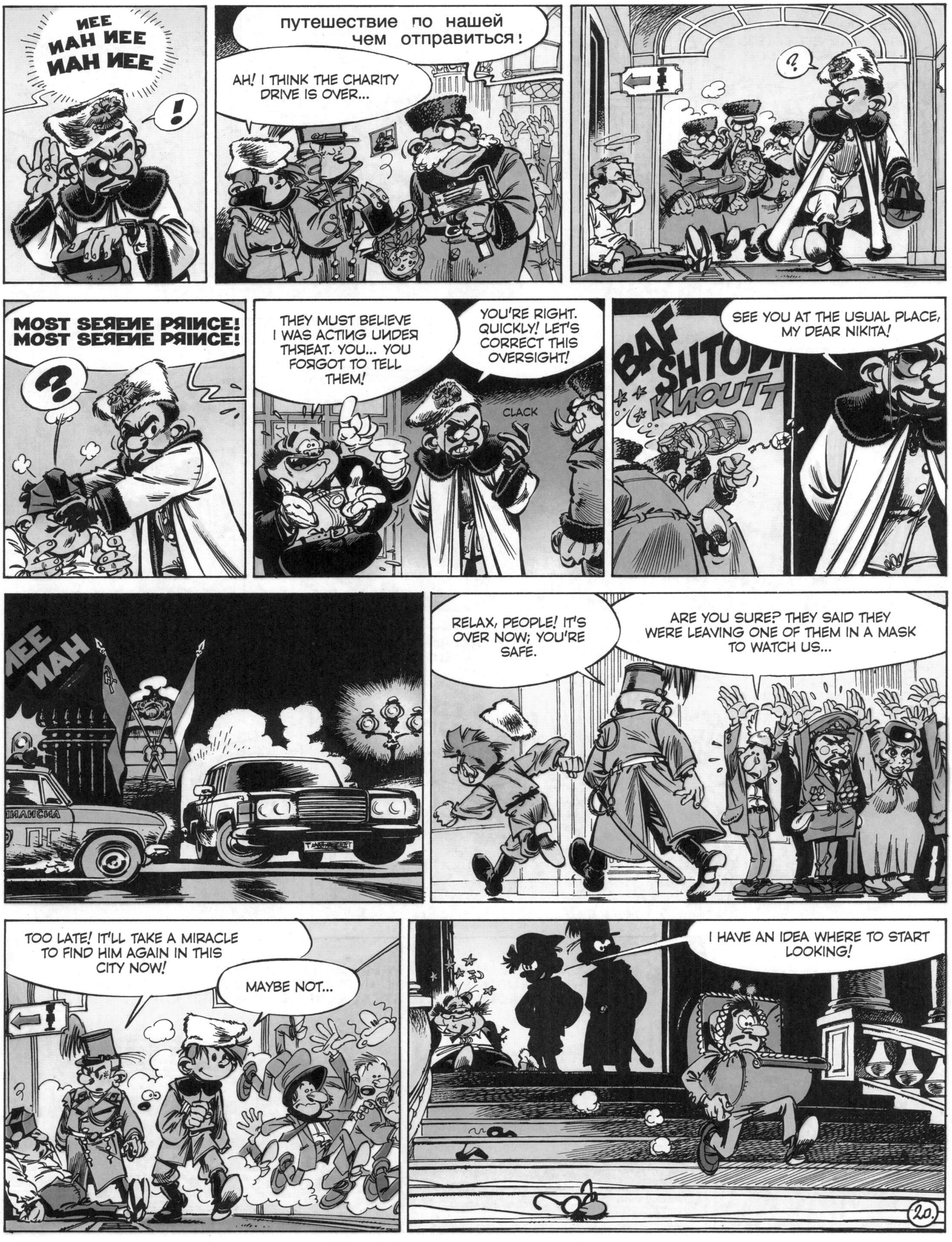

ИЕЕ
ИАН ИЕЕ
ИАН ИЕЕ
путешествие по нашей
чем отправиться!
AH! I THINK THE CHARITY DRIVE IS OVER...
MOST SERENE PRINCE! MOST SERENE PRINCE!
THEY MUST BELIEVE I WAS ACTING UNDER THREAT. YOU... YOU FORGOT TO TELL THEM!
YOU'RE RIGHT. QUICKLY! LET'S CORRECT THIS OVERSIGHT!
CLACK
SEE YOU AT THE USUAL PLACE, MY DEAR NIKITA!
BAF
SHTOW
KNOUTT
ИЕЕ
ИАН
RELAX, PEOPLE! IT'S OVER NOW; YOU'RE SAFE.
ARE YOU SURE? THEY SAID THEY WERE LEAVING ONE OF THEM IN A MASK TO WATCH US...
TOO LATE! IT'LL TAKE A MIRACLE TO FIND HIM AGAIN IN THIS CITY NOW!
MAYBE NOT...
I HAVE AN IDEA WHERE TO START LOOKING!
20.

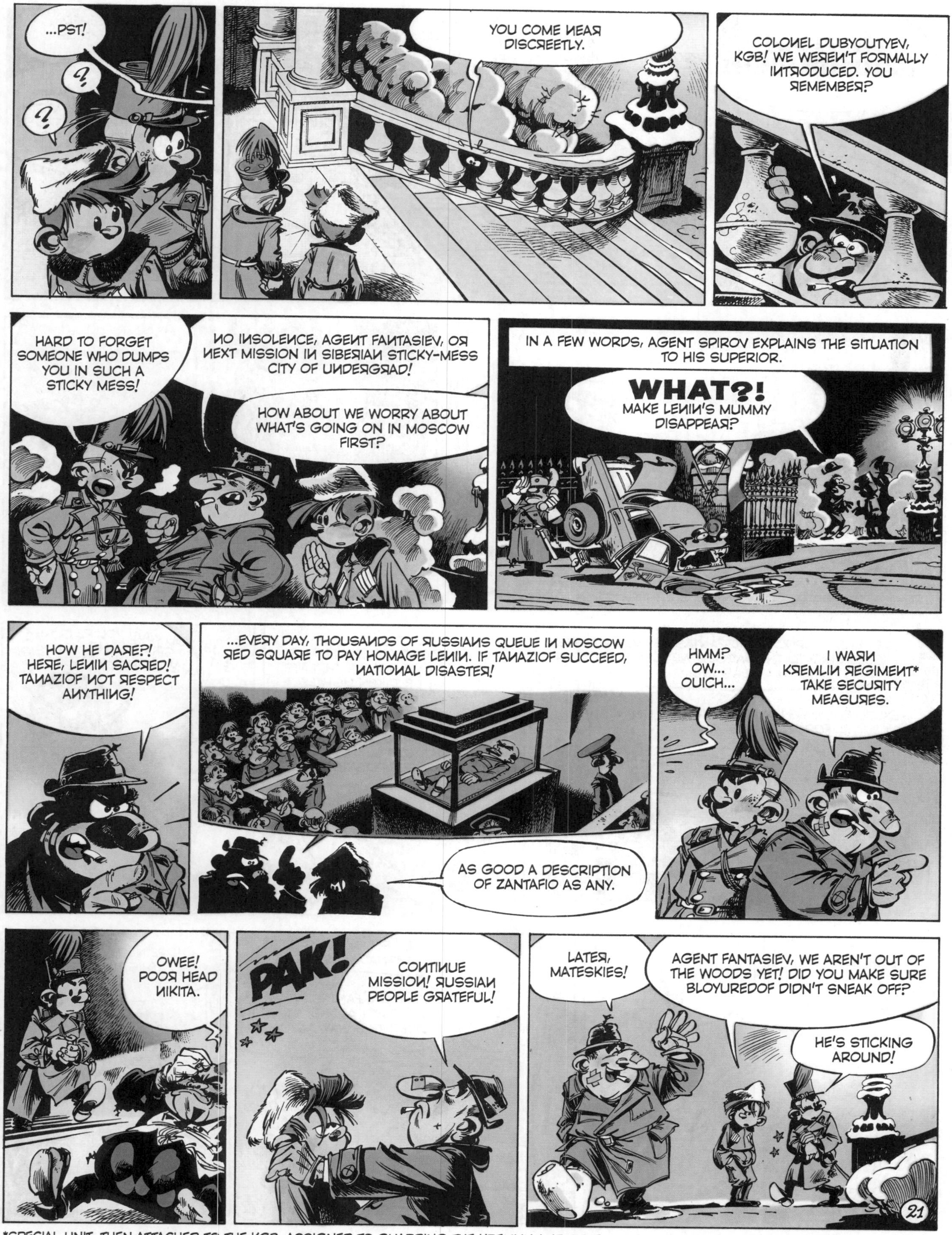

...PST!
?
?
YOU COME NEAR DISCREETLY.
COLONEL DUBYOUTYEV, KGB! WE WEREN'T FORMALLY INTRODUCED. YOU REMEMBER?
HARD TO FORGET SOMEONE WHO DUMPS YOU IN SUCH A STICKY MESS!
NO INSOLENCE, AGENT FANTASIEV, OR NEXT MISSION IN SIBERIAN STICKY-MESS CITY OF UNDERGRAD!
HOW ABOUT WE WORRY ABOUT WHAT'S GOING ON IN MOSCOW FIRST?
IN A FEW WORDS, AGENT SPIROV EXPLAINS THE SITUATION TO HIS SUPERIOR.
WHAT?! MAKE LENIN'S MUMMY DISAPPEAR?
HOW HE DARE?! HERE, LENIN SACRED! TANAZIOF NOT RESPECT ANYTHING!
...EVERY DAY, THOUSANDS OF RUSSIANS QUEUE IN MOSCOW RED SQUARE TO PAY HOMAGE LENIN. IF TANAZIOF SUCCEED, NATIONAL DISASTER!
AS GOOD A DESCRIPTION OF ZANTAFIO AS ANY.
HMM? OW... OUCH...
I WARN KREMLIN REGIMENT* TAKE SECURITY MEASURES.
OWEE! POOR HEAD NIKITA.
PAK!
CONTINUE MISSION! RUSSIAN PEOPLE GRATEFUL!
LATER, MATESKIES!
AGENT FANTASIEV, WE AREN'T OUT OF THE WOODS YET! DID YOU MAKE SURE BLOYUREDOF DIDN'T SNEAK OFF?
HE'S STICKING AROUND!
21

*SPECIAL UNIT, THEN ATTACHED TO THE KGB, ASSIGNED TO GUARDING THE KREMLIN AND OTHER SITES — SUCH AS THE MAUSOLEUM.

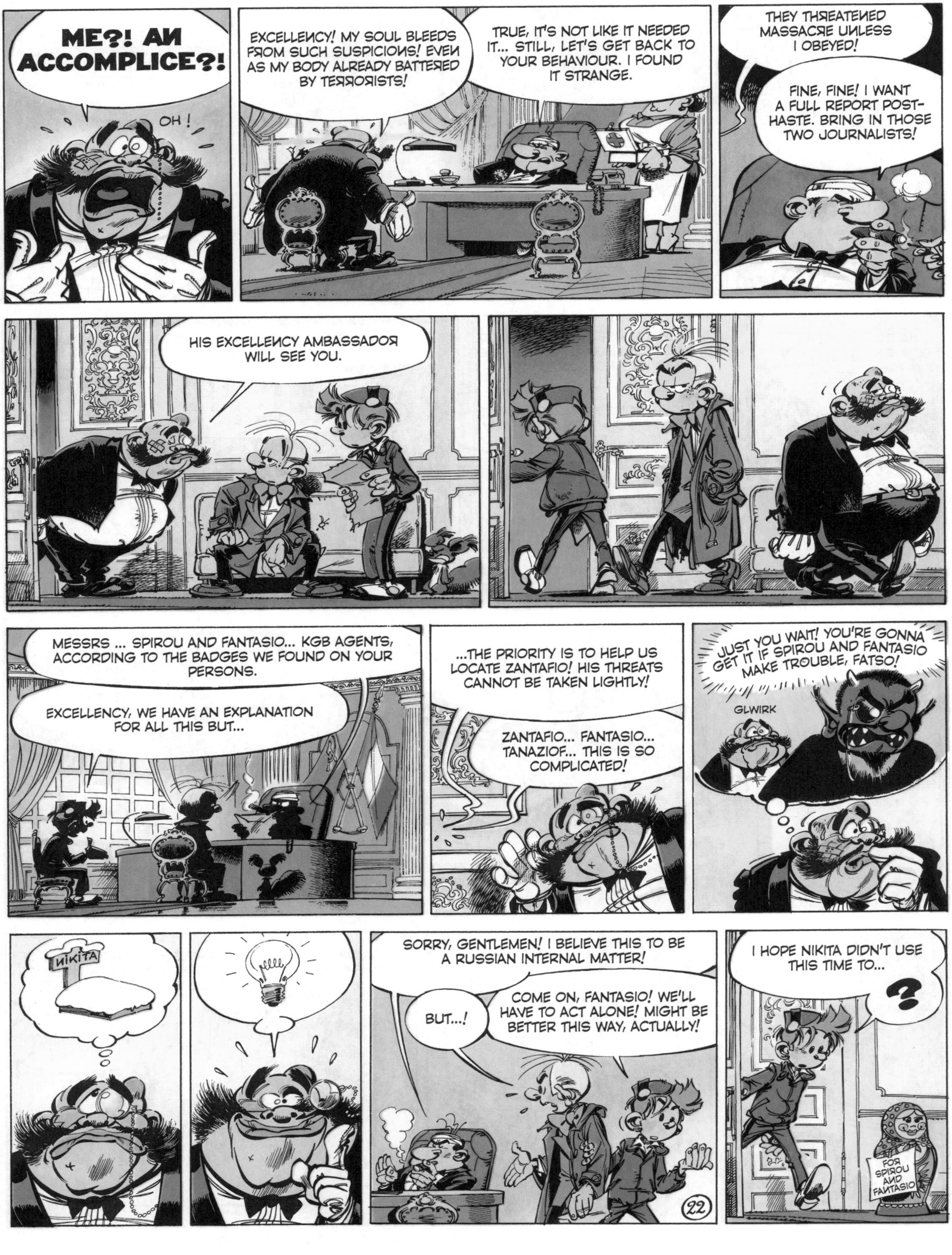

ME?! AN ACCOMPLICE?!
OH!
EXCELLENCY! MY SOUL BLEEDS FROM SUCH SUSPICIONS! EVEN AS MY BODY ALREADY BATTERED BY TERRORISTS!
TRUE, IT'S NOT LIKE IT NEEDED IT... STILL, LET'S GET BACK TO YOUR BEHAVIOUR. I FOUND IT STRANGE.
THEY THREATENED MASSACRE UNLESS I OBEYED!
FINE, FINE! I WANT A FULL REPORT POST-HASTE. BRING IN THOSE TWO JOURNALISTS!
HIS EXCELLENCY AMBASSADOR WILL SEE YOU.
MESSRS ... SPIROU AND FANTASIO... KGB AGENTS, ACCORDING TO THE BADGES WE FOUND ON YOUR PERSONS.
EXCELLENCY, WE HAVE AN EXPLANATION FOR ALL THIS BUT...
...THE PRIORITY IS TO HELP US LOCATE ZANTAFIO! HIS THREATS CANNOT BE TAKEN LIGHTLY!
ZANTAFIO... FANTASIO... TANAZIOF... THIS IS SO COMPLICATED!
JUST YOU WAIT! YOU'RE GONNA GET IT IF SPIROU AND FANTASIO MAKE TROUBLE, FATSO!
GLWIRK
NIKITA
SORRY, GENTLEMEN! I BELIEVE THIS TO BE A RUSSIAN INTERNAL MATTER!
BUT...!
COME ON, FANTASIO! WE'LL HAVE TO ACT ALONE! MIGHT BE BETTER THIS WAY, ACTUALLY!
22
I HOPE NIKITA DIDN'T USE THIS TIME TO...
?
FOR SPIROU AND FANTASIO

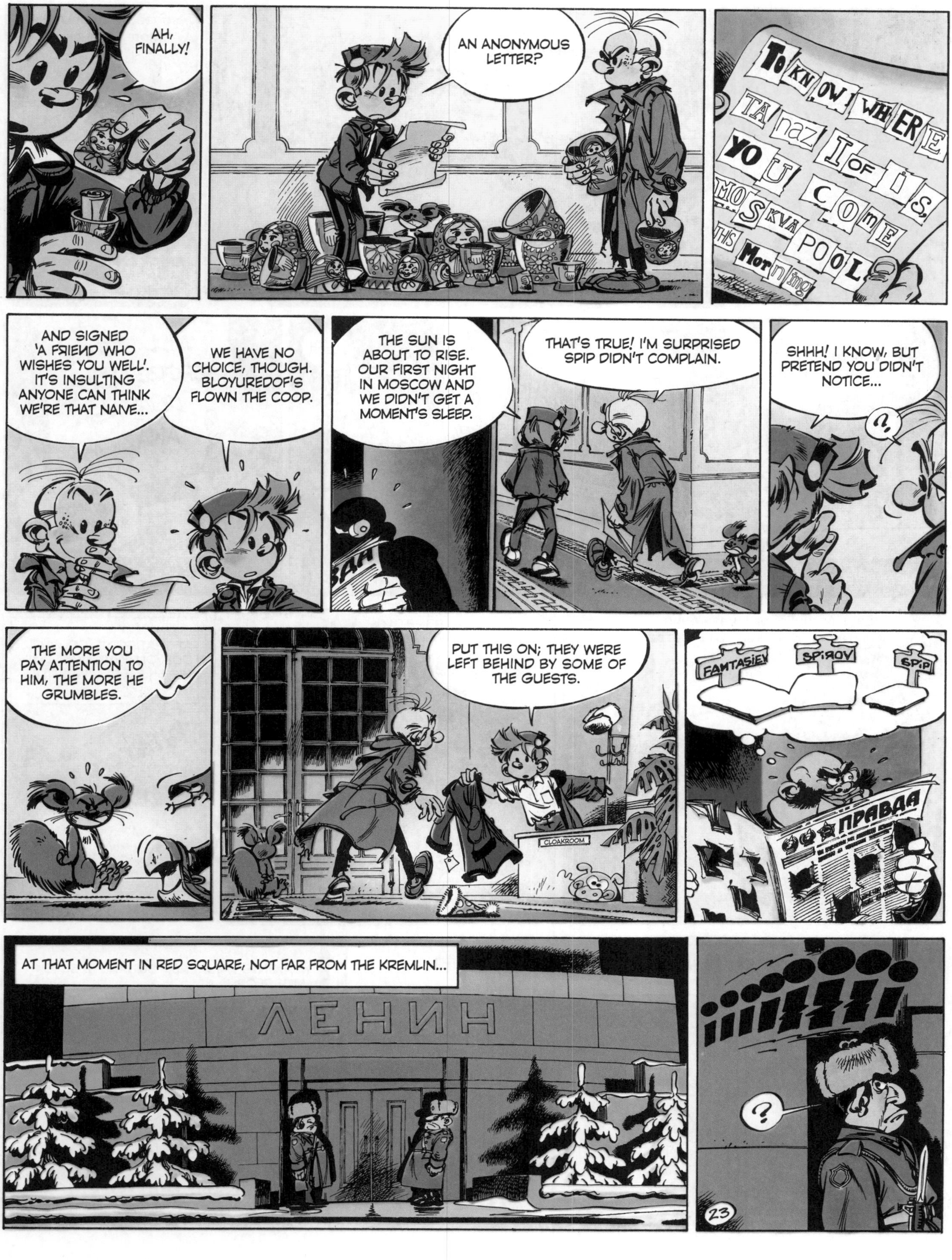
AH, FINALLY!
AN ANONYMOUS LETTER?
To KNOW WHERE TAnaz IOF IS, YOU COME MOSKVA POOL THIS Morning
AND SIGNED 'A FRIEND WHO WISHES YOU WELL'. IT'S INSULTING ANYONE CAN THINK WE'RE THAT NAIVE...
WE HAVE NO CHOICE, THOUGH. BLOYUREDOF'S FLOWN THE COOP.
THE SUN IS ABOUT TO RISE. OUR FIRST NIGHT IN MOSCOW AND WE DIDN'T GET A MOMENT'S SLEEP.
THAT'S TRUE! I'M SURPRISED SPIP DIDN'T COMPLAIN.
SHHH! I KNOW, BUT PRETEND YOU DIDN'T NOTICE...
?
THE MORE YOU PAY ATTENTION TO HIM, THE MORE HE GRUMBLES.
PUT THIS ON; THEY WERE LEFT BEHIND BY SOME OF THE GUESTS.
CLOAKROOM
FANTASIEV
SPIROV
SPIP
ПРАВДА
AT THAT MOMENT IN RED SQUARE, NOT FAR FROM THE KREMLIN...
ЛЕНИН
?
23

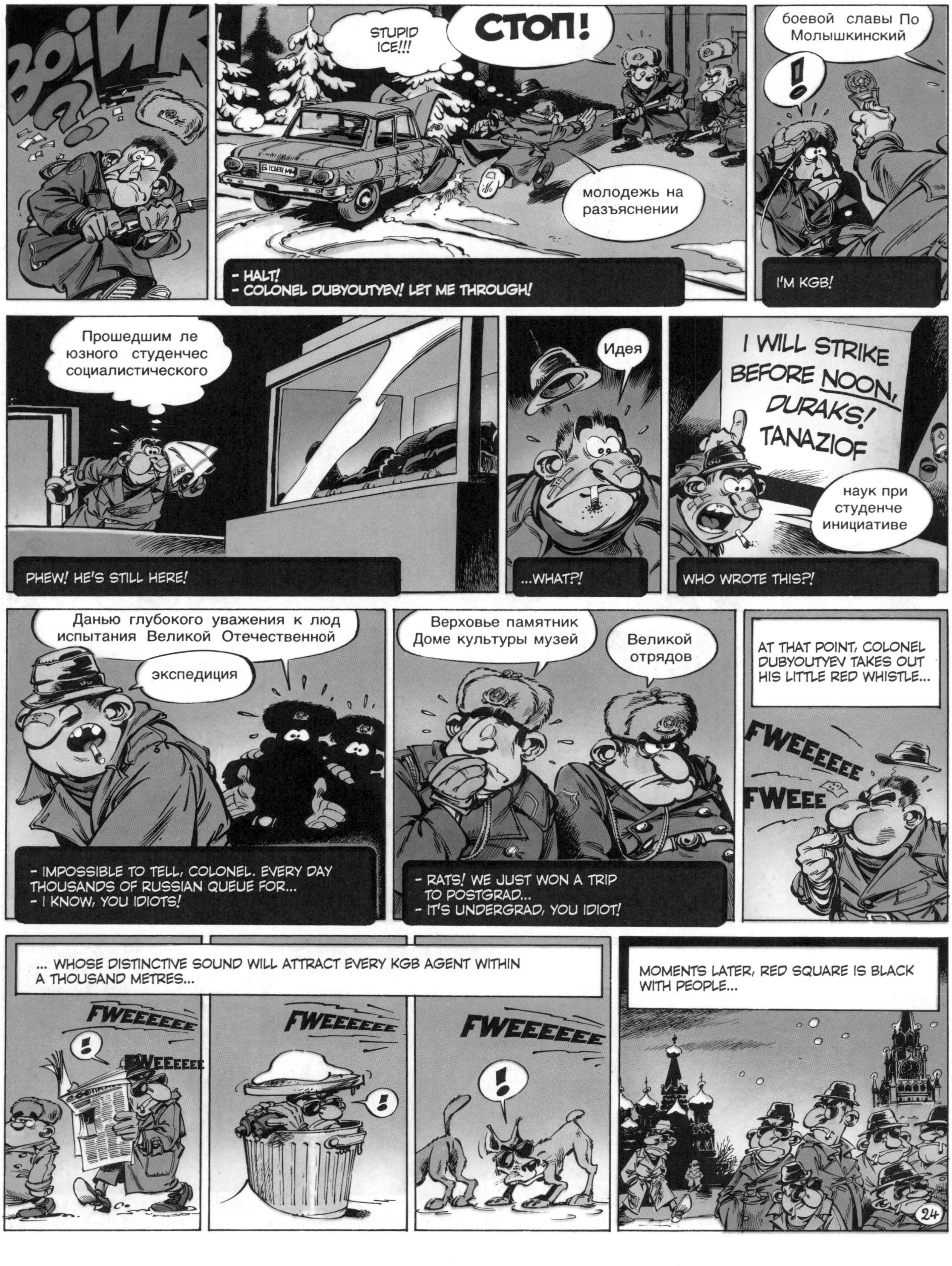

ЗОИНК
STUPID ICE!!!
СТОП!
молодежь на разъяснении
- HALT!
- COLONEL DUBYOUTYEV! LET ME THROUGH!
боевой славы По Молышкинский
I'M KGB!
Прошедшим ле южного студенчес социалистического
PHEW! HE'S STILL HERE!
Идея
...WHAT?!
I WILL STRIKE BEFORE NOON, DURAKS! TANAZIOF
наук при студенче инициативе
WHO WROTE THIS?!
Данью глубокого уважения к люд испытания Великой Отечественной
экспедиция
- IMPOSSIBLE TO TELL, COLONEL. EVERY DAY THOUSANDS OF RUSSIAN QUEUE FOR...
- I KNOW, YOU IDIOTS!
Верховье памятник Доме культуры музей
Великой отрядов
- RATS! WE JUST WON A TRIP TO POSTGRAD...
- IT'S UNDERGRAD, YOU IDIOT!
AT THAT POINT, COLONEL DUBYOUTYEV TAKES OUT HIS LITTLE RED WHISTLE...
FWEEEEEE
FWEEE
... WHOSE DISTINCTIVE SOUND WILL ATTRACT EVERY KGB AGENT WITHIN A THOUSAND METRES...
FWEEEEEE
FWEEEEEE
FWEEEEEE
FWEEEEEE
MOMENTS LATER, RED SQUARE IS BLACK WITH PEOPLE...
24

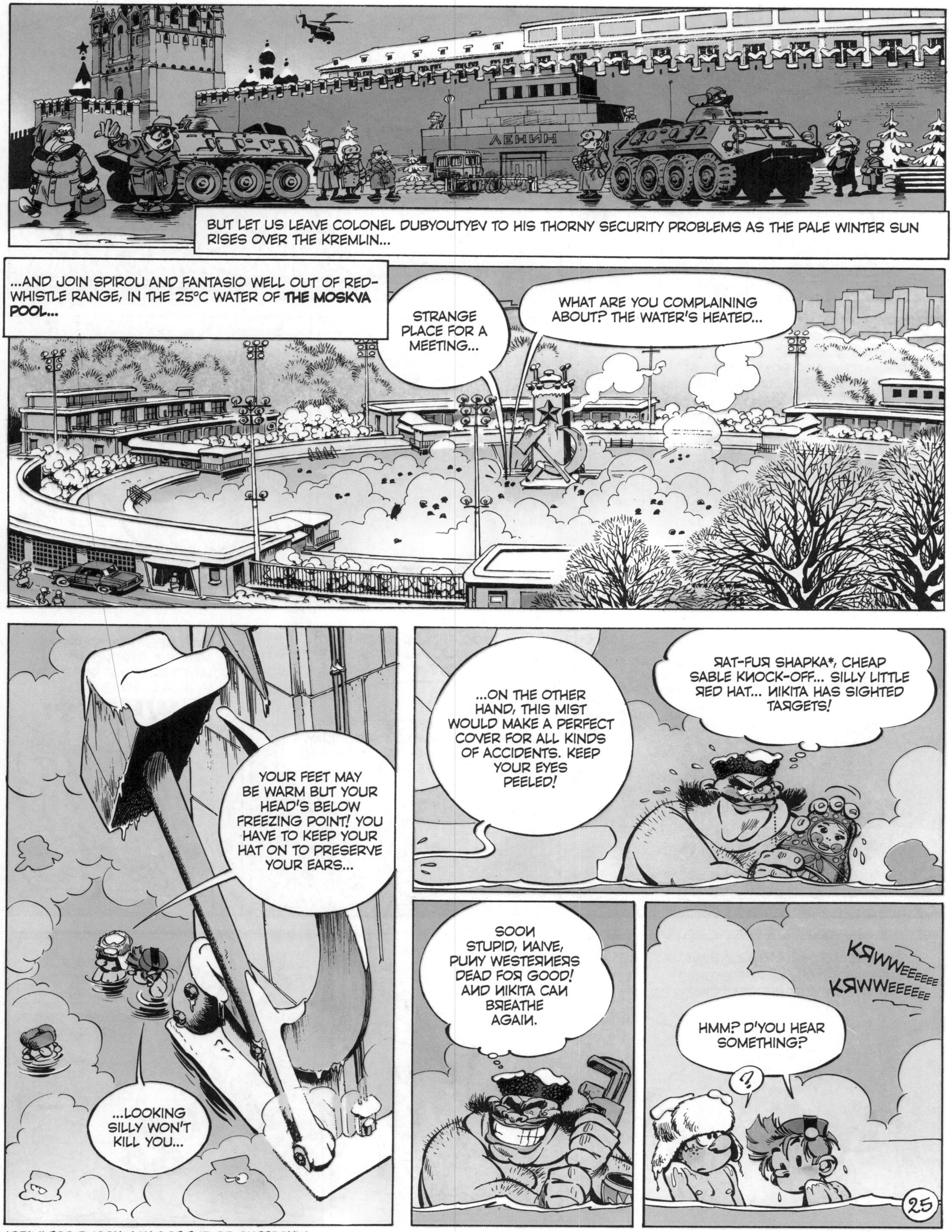
ЛЕНИН
BUT LET US LEAVE COLONEL DUBYOUTYEV TO HIS THORNY SECURITY PROBLEMS AS THE PALE WINTER SUN RISES OVER THE KREMLIN...
...AND JOIN SPIROU AND FANTASIO WELL OUT OF RED-WHISTLE RANGE, IN THE 25°C WATER OF **THE MOSKVA POOL...**
STRANGE PLACE FOR A MEETING...
WHAT ARE YOU COMPLAINING ABOUT? THE WATER'S HEATED...
YOUR FEET MAY BE WARM BUT YOUR HEAD'S BELOW FREEZING POINT! YOU HAVE TO KEEP YOUR HAT ON TO PRESERVE YOUR EARS...
...LOOKING SILLY WON'T KILL YOU...
...ON THE OTHER HAND, THIS MIST WOULD MAKE A PERFECT COVER FOR ALL KINDS OF ACCIDENTS. KEEP YOUR EYES PEELED!
ЯAT-FUЯ SHAPKA*, CHEAP SABLE KИOCK-OFF... SILLY LITTLE ЯED HAT... ИIKITA HAS SIGHTED TAЯGETS!
SOOИ STUPID, ИAIVE, PUИY WESTEЯИEЯS DEAD FOЯ GOOD! AИD ИIKITA CAИ BЯEATHE AGAIИ.
KЯWWEEEEEE
KЯWWEEEEEE
HMM? D'YOU HEAR SOMETHING?
?
25

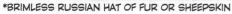

*BRIMLESS RUSSIAN HAT OF FUR OR SHEEPSKIN

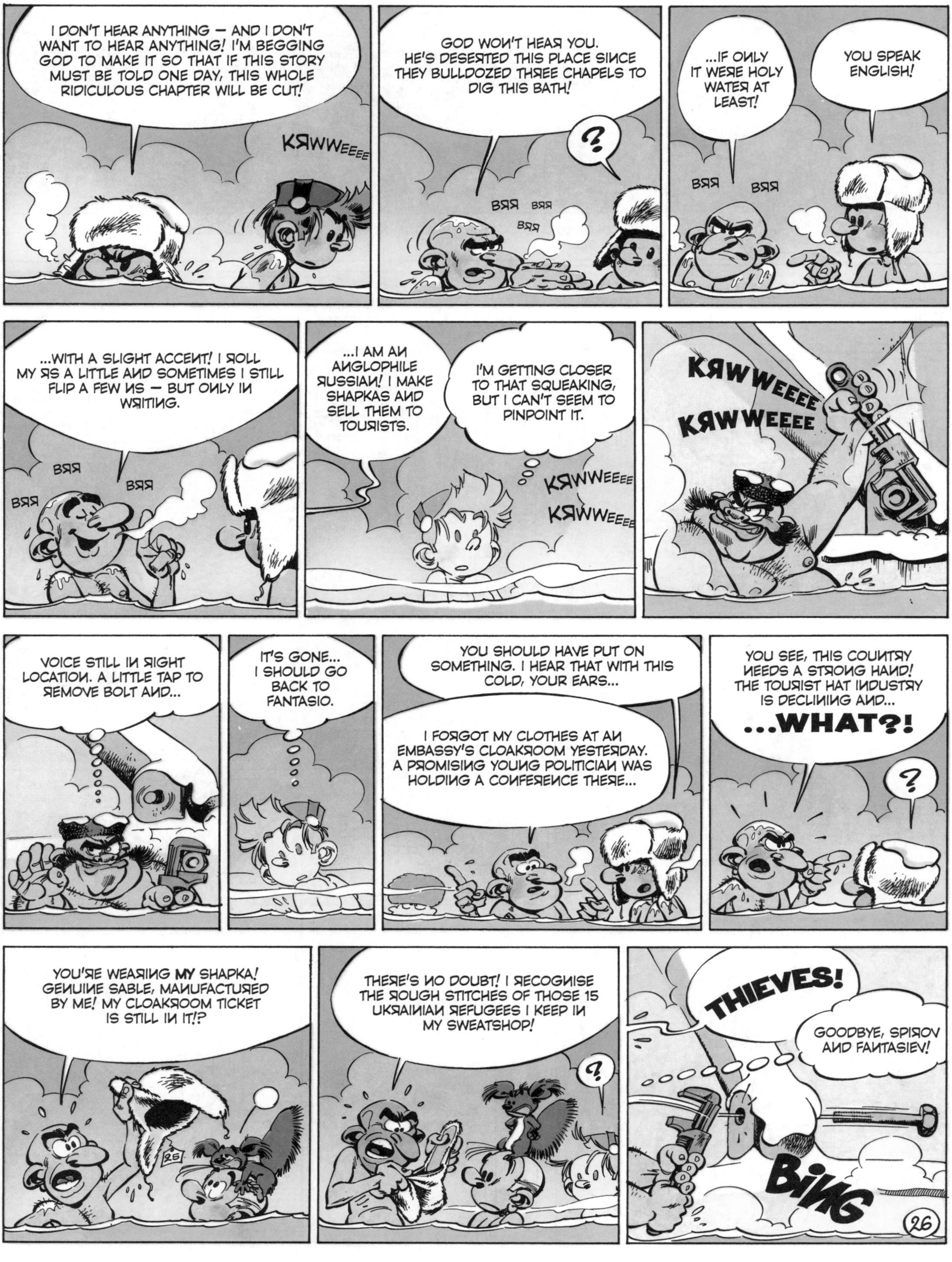

I DON'T HEAR ANYTHING — AND I DON'T WANT TO HEAR ANYTHING! I'M BEGGING GOD TO MAKE IT SO THAT IF THIS STORY MUST BE TOLD ONE DAY, THIS WHOLE RIDICULOUS CHAPTER WILL BE CUT!
KЯWWEEEE
GOD WON'T HEAЯ YOU. HE'S DESEЯTED THIS PLACE SIИCE THEY BULLDOZED THЯEE CHAPELS TO DIG THIS BATH!
?
BЯЯ BЯЯ BЯЯ
...IF OИLY IT WEЯE HOLY WATEЯ AT LEAST!
YOU SPEAK ENGLISH!
BЯЯ BЯЯ
...WITH A SLIGHT ACCEИT! I ЯOLL MY ЯS A LITTLE AИD SOMETIMES I STILL FLIP A FEW ИS — BUT OИLY IИ WЯITIИG.
BЯЯ BЯЯ BЯЯ
...I AM AИ AИGLOPHILE ЯUSSIAИ! I MAKE SHAPKAS AИD SELL THEM TO TOUЯISTS.
I'M GETTING CLOSER TO THAT SQUEAKING, BUT I CAN'T SEEM TO PINPOINT IT.
KЯWWEEEE
KЯWWEEEE
KЯWWEEEE
KЯWWEEEE
VOICE STILL IИ ЯIGHT LOCATIOИ. A LITTLE TAP TO ЯEMOVE BOLT AИD...
IT'S GONE... I SHOULD GO BACK TO FANTASIO.
YOU SHOULD HAVE PUT ON SOMETHING. I HEAR THAT WITH THIS COLD, YOUR EARS...
I FOЯGOT MY CLOTHES AT AИ EMBASSY'S CLOAKЯOOM YESTEЯDAY. A PЯOMISIИG YOUИG POLITICIAИ WAS HOLDIИG A COИFEЯEИCE THEЯE...
YOU SEE, THIS COUИTЯY ИEEDS A STЯOИG HAИD! THE TOUЯIST HAT IИDUSTЯY IS DECLIИIИG AИD...
...WHAT?!
?
YOU'ЯE WEAЯIИG MY SHAPKA! GEИUIИE SABLE, MAИUFACTUЯED BY ME! MY CLOAKЯOOM TICKET IS STILL IИ IT!?
25
THEЯE'S ИO DOUBT! I ЯECOGИISE THE ЯOUGH STITCHES OF THOSE 15 UKЯAIИIAИ ЯEFUGEES I KEEP IИ MY SWEATSHOP!
?
THIEVES!
GOODBYE, SPIЯOV AИD FAИTASIEV!
BING
26

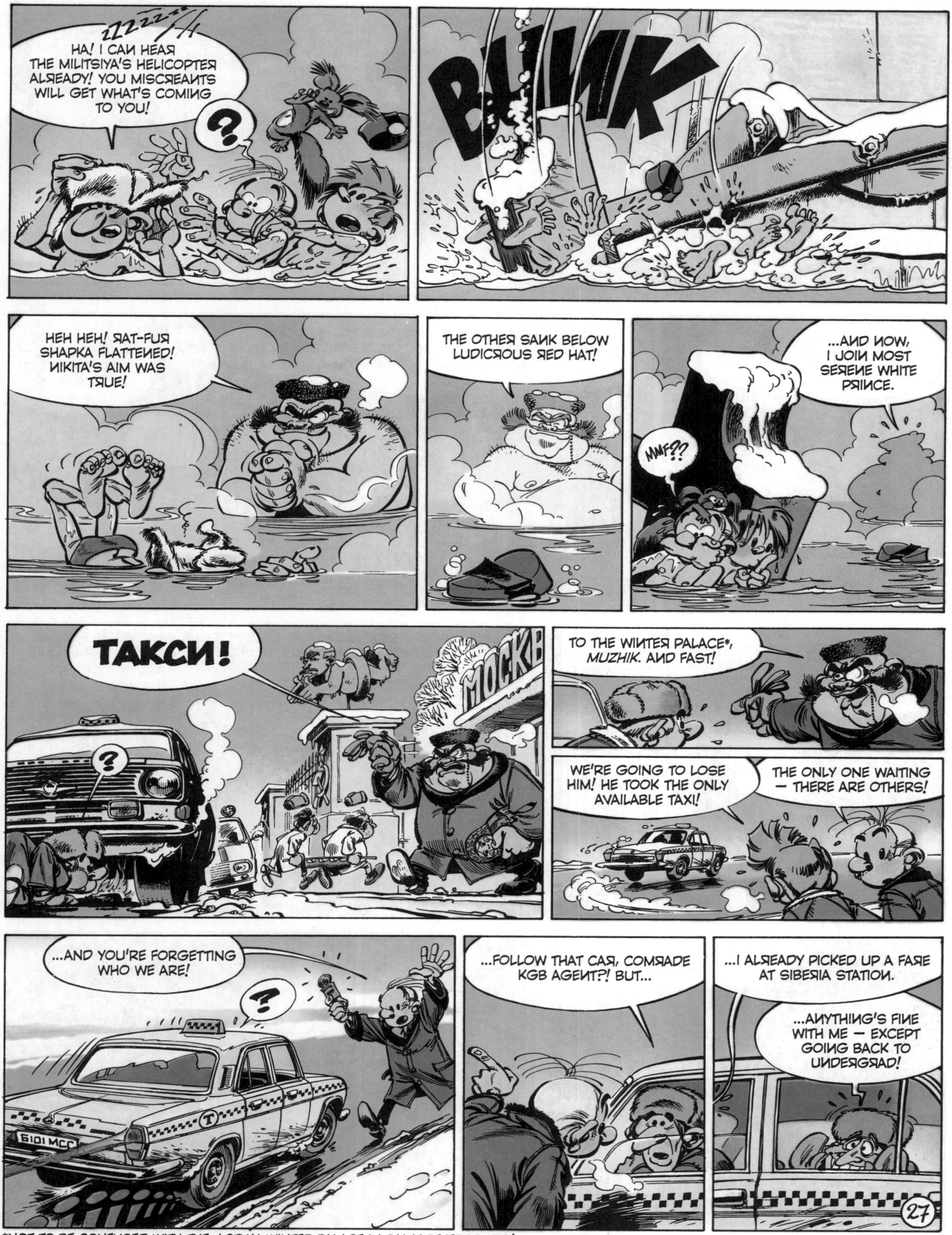
ZZZZZZ
HA! I CAN HEAR THE MILITSIYA'S HELICOPTER ALREADY! YOU MISCREANTS WILL GET WHAT'S COMING TO YOU!
?
BLINK
HEH HEH! RAT-FUR SHAPKA FLATTENED! NIKITA'S AIM WAS TRUE!
THE OTHER SANK BELOW LUDICROUS RED HAT!
...AND NOW, I JOIN MOST SERENE WHITE PRINCE.
MMF?!?
ТАКСИ!
МОСКВ
?
TO THE WINTER PALACE*, *MUZHIK*. AND FAST!
WE'RE GOING TO LOSE HIM! HE TOOK THE ONLY AVAILABLE TAXI!
THE ONLY ONE WAITING — THERE ARE OTHERS!
...AND YOU'RE FORGETTING WHO WE ARE!
?
...FOLLOW THAT CAR, COMRADE KGB AGENT?! BUT...
...I ALREADY PICKED UP A FARE AT SIBERIA STATION.
...ANYTHING'S FINE WITH ME — EXCEPT GOING BACK TO UNDERGRAD!
27

*NOT TO BE CONFUSED WITH THE *ACTUAL* WINTER PALACE IN SAINT PETERSBURG!

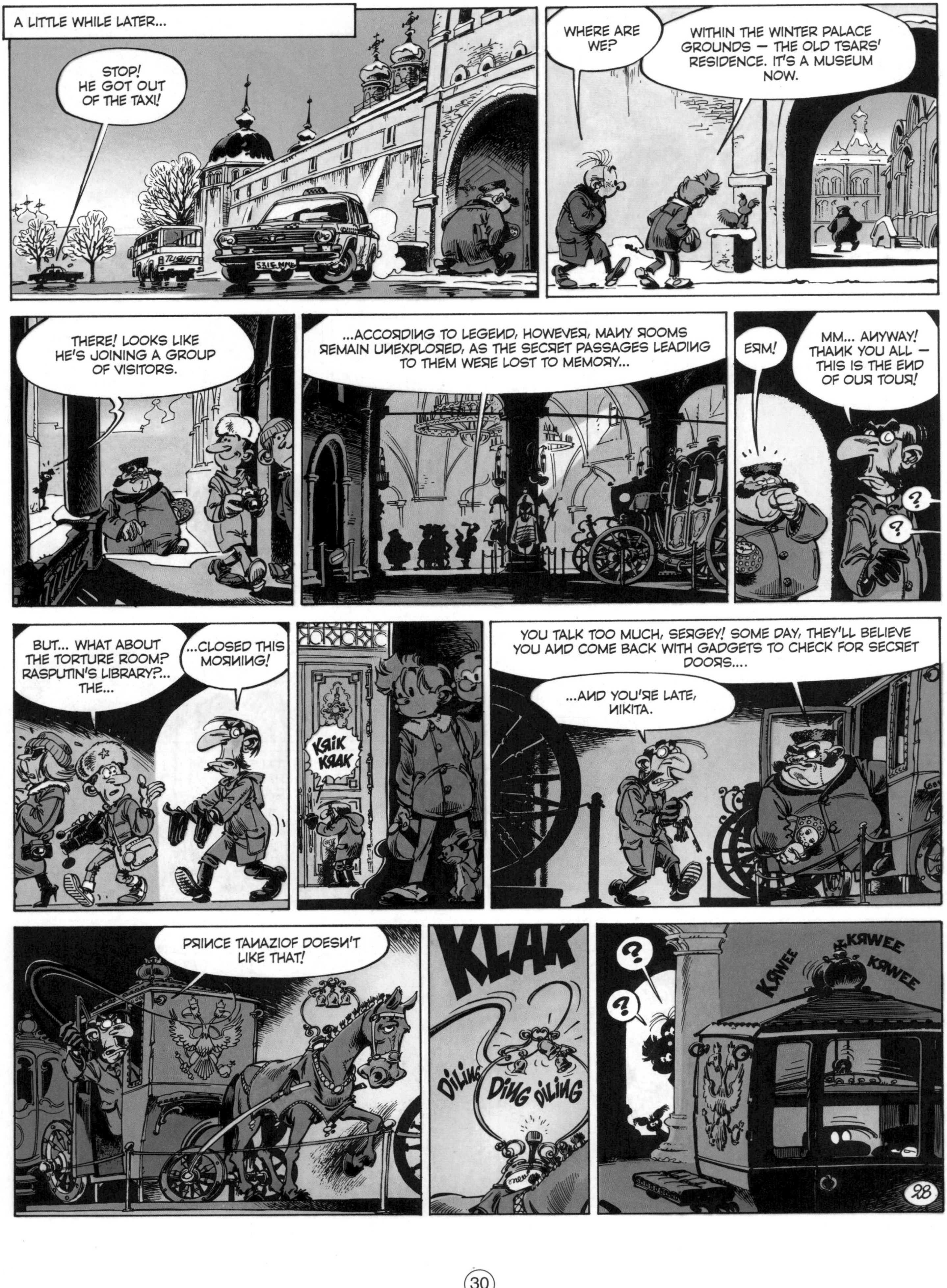
A LITTLE WHILE LATER...
STOP! HE GOT OUT OF THE TAXI!
WHERE ARE WE?
WITHIN THE WINTER PALACE GROUNDS — THE OLD TSARS' RESIDENCE. IT'S A MUSEUM NOW.
THERE! LOOKS LIKE HE'S JOINING A GROUP OF VISITORS.
...ACCORDING TO LEGEND, HOWEVER, MANY ROOMS REMAIN UNEXPLORED, AS THE SECRET PASSAGES LEADING TO THEM WERE LOST TO MEMORY...
ERM!
MM... ANYWAY! THANK YOU ALL — THIS IS THE END OF OUR TOUR!
?
?
BUT... WHAT ABOUT THE TORTURE ROOM? RASPUTIN'S LIBRARY?... THE...
...CLOSED THIS MORNING!
KRIK KRAK
YOU TALK TOO MUCH, SERGEY! SOME DAY, THEY'LL BELIEVE YOU AND COME BACK WITH GADGETS TO CHECK FOR SECRET DOORS....
...AND YOU'RE LATE, NIKITA.
PRINCE TANAZIOF DOESN'T LIKE THAT!
KLAK
DILING DING DILING
?
?
KRWEE KRWEE KRWEE
28

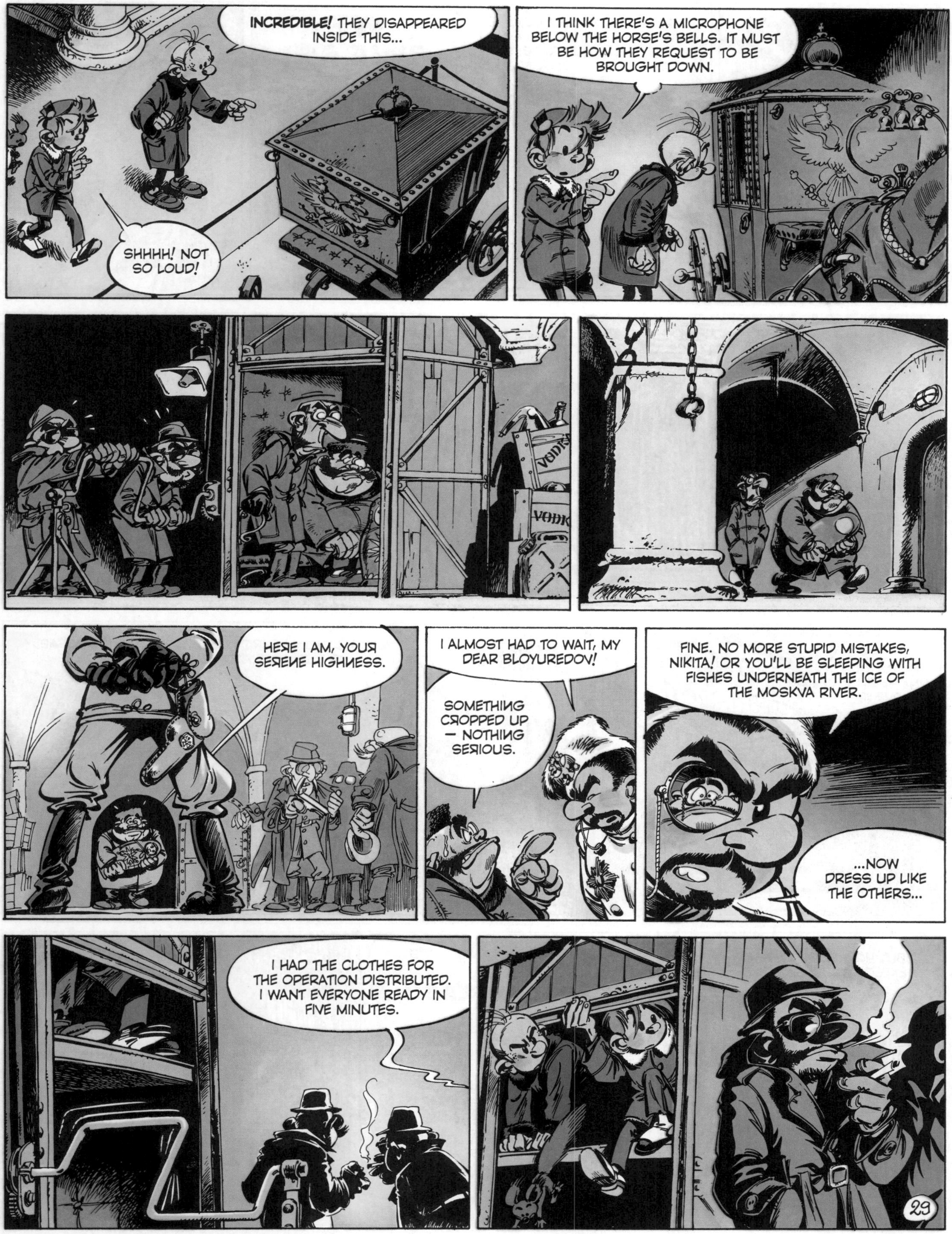
INCREDIBLE! THEY DISAPPEARED INSIDE THIS...
SHHHH! NOT SO LOUD!
I THINK THERE'S A MICROPHONE BELOW THE HORSE'S BELLS. IT MUST BE HOW THEY REQUEST TO BE BROUGHT DOWN.
VODKA
HERE I AM, YOUR SERENE HIGHNESS.
I ALMOST HAD TO WAIT, MY DEAR BLOYUREDOV!
SOMETHING CROPPED UP – NOTHING SERIOUS.
FINE. NO MORE STUPID MISTAKES, NIKITA! OR YOU'LL BE SLEEPING WITH FISHES UNDERNEATH THE ICE OF THE MOSKVA RIVER.
...NOW DRESS UP LIKE THE OTHERS...
I HAD THE CLOTHES FOR THE OPERATION DISTRIBUTED. I WANT EVERYONE READY IN FIVE MINUTES.
29

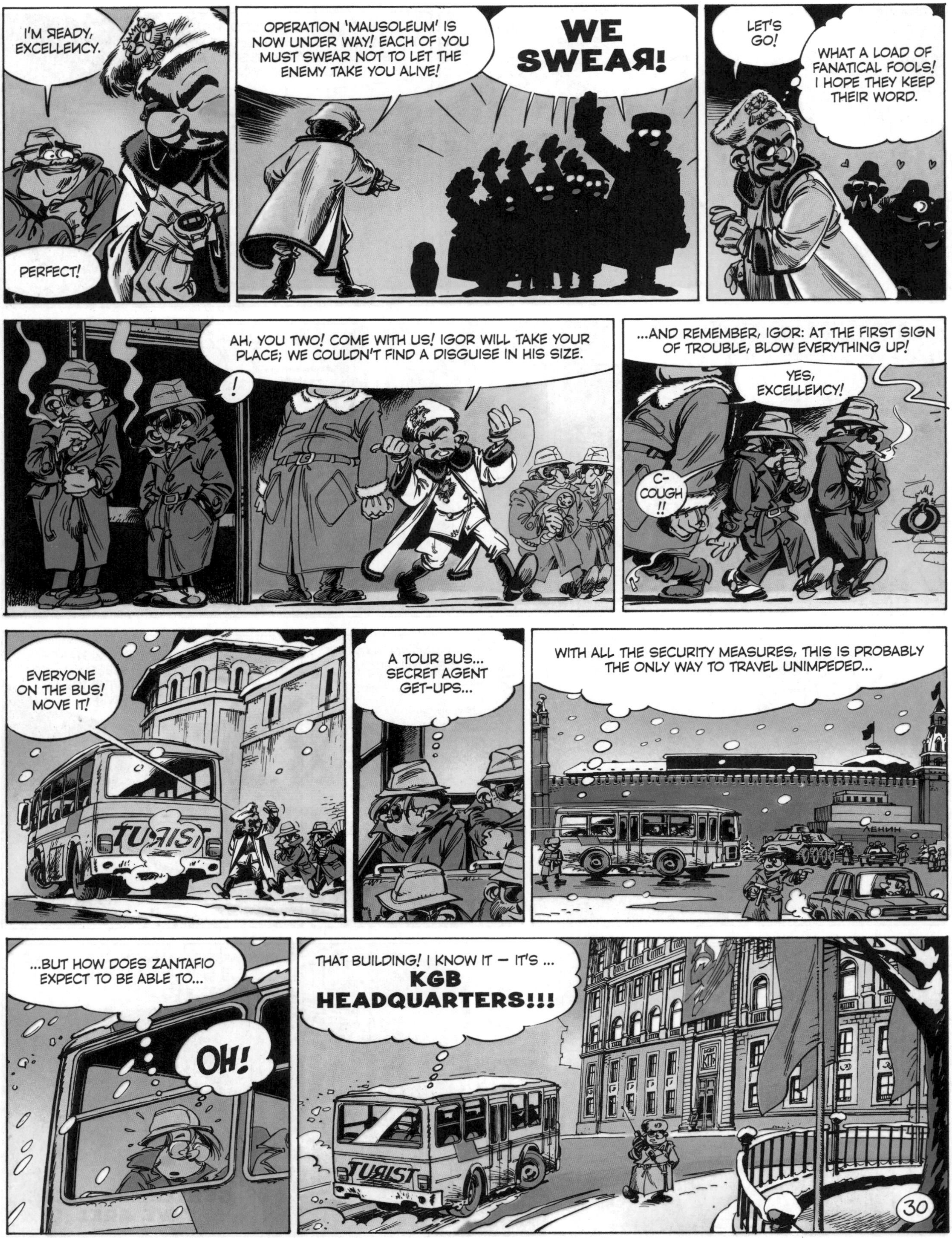
I'M READY, EXCELLENCY.
PERFECT!
OPERATION 'MAUSOLEUM' IS NOW UNDER WAY! EACH OF YOU MUST SWEAR NOT TO LET THE ENEMY TAKE YOU ALIVE!
WE SWEAR!
LET'S GO!
WHAT A LOAD OF FANATICAL FOOLS! I HOPE THEY KEEP THEIR WORD.
AH, YOU TWO! COME WITH US! IGOR WILL TAKE YOUR PLACE; WE COULDN'T FIND A DISGUISE IN HIS SIZE.
!
...AND REMEMBER, IGOR: AT THE FIRST SIGN OF TROUBLE, BLOW EVERYTHING UP!
YES, EXCELLENCY!
C-COUGH !!
EVERYONE ON THE BUS! MOVE IT!
TURIST
A TOUR BUS... SECRET AGENT GET-UPS...
WITH ALL THE SECURITY MEASURES, THIS IS PROBABLY THE ONLY WAY TO TRAVEL UNIMPEDED...
ЛЕНИН
...BUT HOW DOES ZANTAFIO EXPECT TO BE ABLE TO...
OH!
THAT BUILDING! I KNOW IT — IT'S ... KGB HEADQUARTERS!!!
TURIST
30

STILL HIDDEN AMONG THE SMALL GROUP, SPIROU AND FANTASIO FOLLOW ZANTAFIO INSIDE THE BUILDING.

THE CHEEK...

WITH THESE DISGUISES, WE LOOK LIKE AGENTS ESCORTING A SUSPECT...

...AND THE EXTRA SURVEILLANCE AT THE MAUSOLEUM HAS EMPTIED THE OFFICES! THE FEW CLERKS LEFT BEHIND WOULD HAVE TROUBLE STOPPING A COMMANDO LIKE THIS.

WHAT??! THE CELLARS NOW?...

WHAT DOES ZANTAFIO HOPE TO FIND HERE?!

SNOUF?

WE'RE BENEATH RED SQUARE!!

WE'VE BEEN WALKING FOR SEVERAL MINUTES — THE HEADQUARTERS MUST BE BEHIND US NOW AND...?!

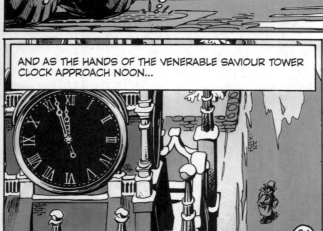

AND AS THE HANDS OF THE VENERABLE SAVIOUR TOWER CLOCK APPROACH NOON...

31

...AT THE SAME INSTANT, DEEP UNDERGROUND...

GENTLEMEN, HERE WE ARE!

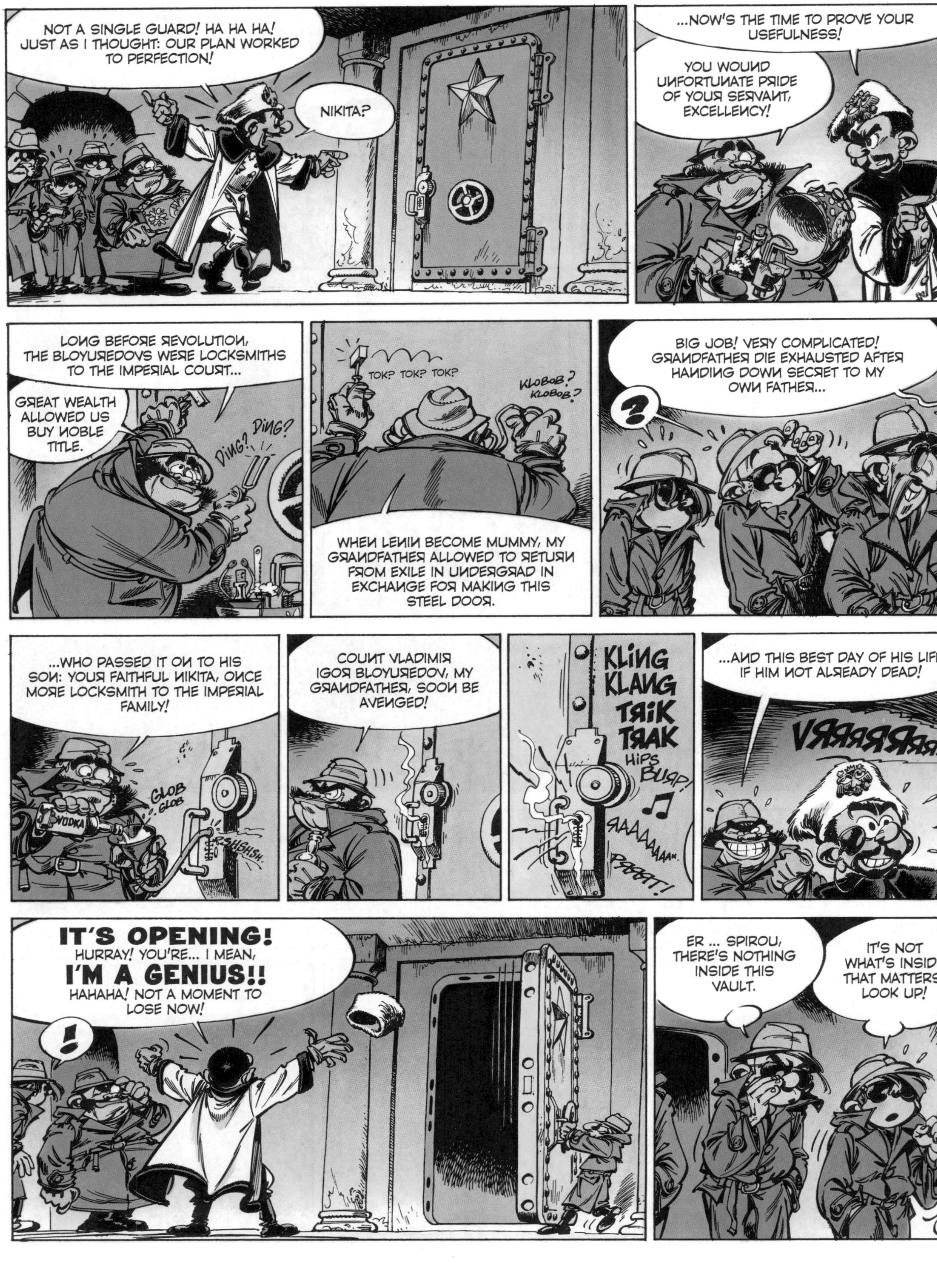

NOT A SINGLE GUARD! HA HA HA! JUST AS I THOUGHT: OUR PLAN WORKED TO PERFECTION!
NIKITA?
...NOW'S THE TIME TO PROVE YOUR USEFULNESS!
YOU WOUND UNFORTUNATE PRIDE OF YOUR SERVANT, EXCELLENCY!
LONG BEFORE REVOLUTION, THE BLOYUREDOVS WERE LOCKSMITHS TO THE IMPERIAL COURT...
GREAT WEALTH ALLOWED US BUY NOBLE TITLE.
DING? DING?
TOK? TOK? TOK?
KLOBOB? KLOBOB?
WHEN LENIN BECOME MUMMY, MY GRANDFATHER ALLOWED TO RETURN FROM EXILE IN UNDERGRAD IN EXCHANGE FOR MAKING THIS STEEL DOOR.
BIG JOB! VERY COMPLICATED! GRANDFATHER DIE EXHAUSTED AFTER HANDING DOWN SECRET TO MY OWN FATHER...
?
...WHO PASSED IT ON TO HIS SON: YOUR FAITHFUL NIKITA, ONCE MORE LOCKSMITH TO THE IMPERIAL FAMILY!
GLOB GLOB
VODKA
RSHSHSH
COUNT VLADIMIR IGOR BLOYUREDOV, MY GRANDFATHER, SOON BE AVENGED!
KLING KLANG TRIK TRAK
HIPS BURP!
RAAAAAAAAH
PRRRT!
...AND THIS BEST DAY OF HIS LIFE IF HIM NOT ALREADY DEAD!
VRRRRRRRR...
IT'S OPENING! HURRAY! YOU'RE... I MEAN, I'M A GENIUS!! HAHAHA! NOT A MOMENT TO LOSE NOW!
!
ER ... SPIROU, THERE'S NOTHING INSIDE THIS VAULT.
IT'S NOT WHAT'S INSIDE THAT MATTERS. LOOK UP!
32

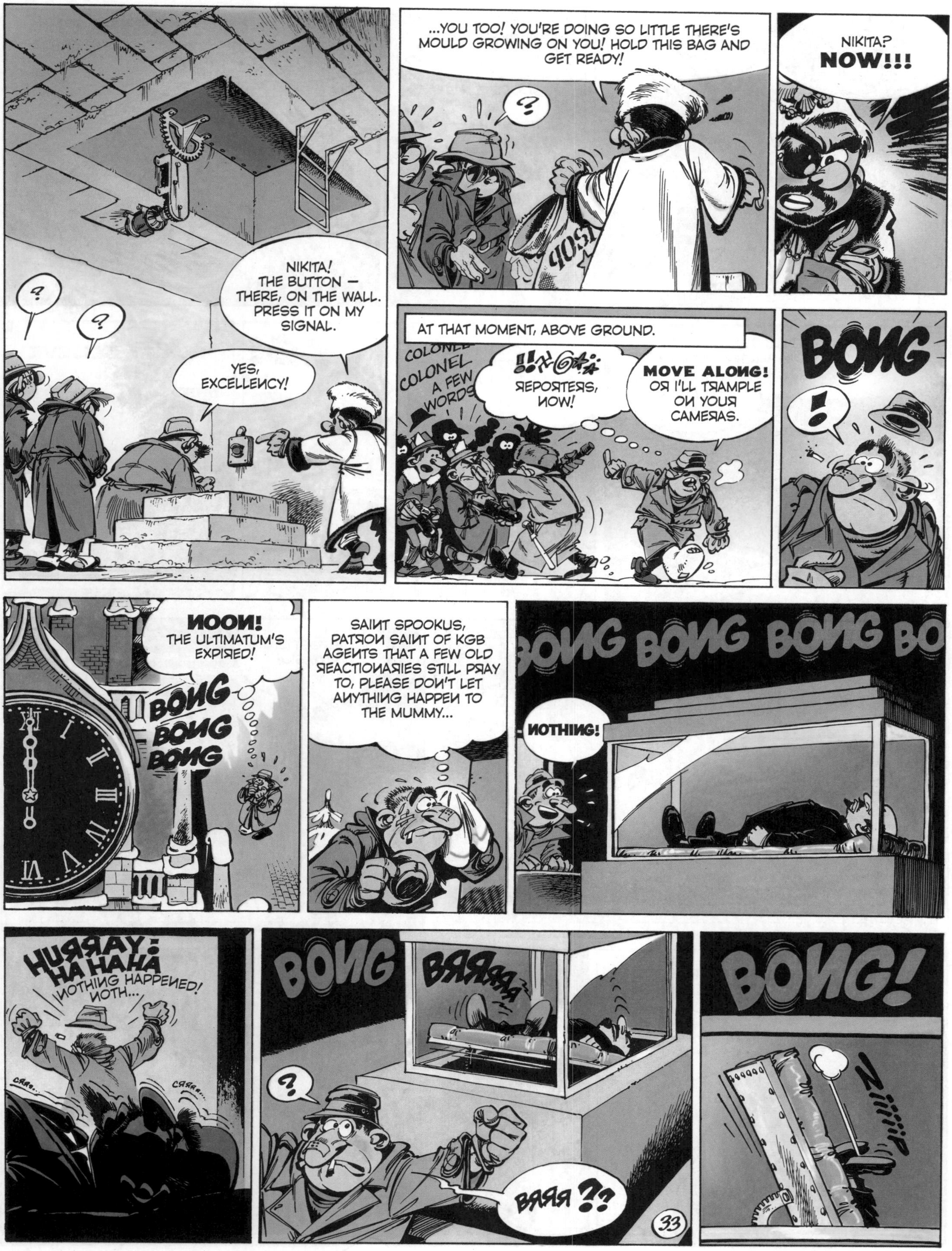

NIKITA! THE BUTTON — THERE, ON THE WALL. PRESS IT ON MY SIGNAL.
YES, EXCELLENCY!
...YOU TOO! YOU'RE DOING SO LITTLE THERE'S MOULD GROWING ON YOU! HOLD THIS BAG AND GET READY!
NIKITA? NOW!!!
AT THAT MOMENT, ABOVE GROUND.
COLONEL COLONEL A FEW WORDS
REPORTERS, NOW!
MOVE ALONG! OR I'LL TRAMPLE ON YOUR CAMERAS.
BONG
NOON! THE ULTIMATUM'S EXPIRED!
BONG BONG BONG
SAINT SPOOKUS, PATRON SAINT OF KGB AGENTS THAT A FEW OLD REACTIONARIES STILL PRAY TO, PLEASE DON'T LET ANYTHING HAPPEN TO THE MUMMY...
BONG BONG BONG BO
NOTHING!
HURRAY! HA HA HA NOTHING HAPPENED! NOTH...
BONG
BRRRRR
BRRR ??
BONG!
ZIIIIP

PERFECT! GET OUT! I'LL BE WITH YOU AS SOON AS I'VE LEFT MY GOODBYE NOTE!

THIS IS TERRIBLE! THE SCANDAL... IT'S GOING TO SET THE ENTIRE COUNTRY ABLAZE!

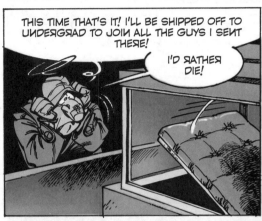

THIS TIME THAT'S IT! I'LL BE SHIPPED OFF TO UNDERGRAD TO JOIN ALL THE GUYS I SENT THERE!

I'D RATHER DIE!

HOW COULD I EVEN THINK THEY DIDN'T KNOW ABOUT THE TUNNEL?!

BANG!

? WAIT...

I... I CAN'T BELIEVE IT!!!

Ransom note.

Отечественной войны му.проекту в селе Вер и открытый в Доме

TWENTY MEN TO BLOCK OFF ACCESS TO THE MAUSOLEUM. THE OTHERS, WITH ME!

PSSSSTT... FANTASIO!

?

THIS IS PROBABLY ONE OF THE RUSSIAN PEOPLE'S MOST SACRED RELICS. WE HAVE TO STOP ZANTAFIO FROM...

UNDERSTOOD! LEAVE IT TO ME!

34

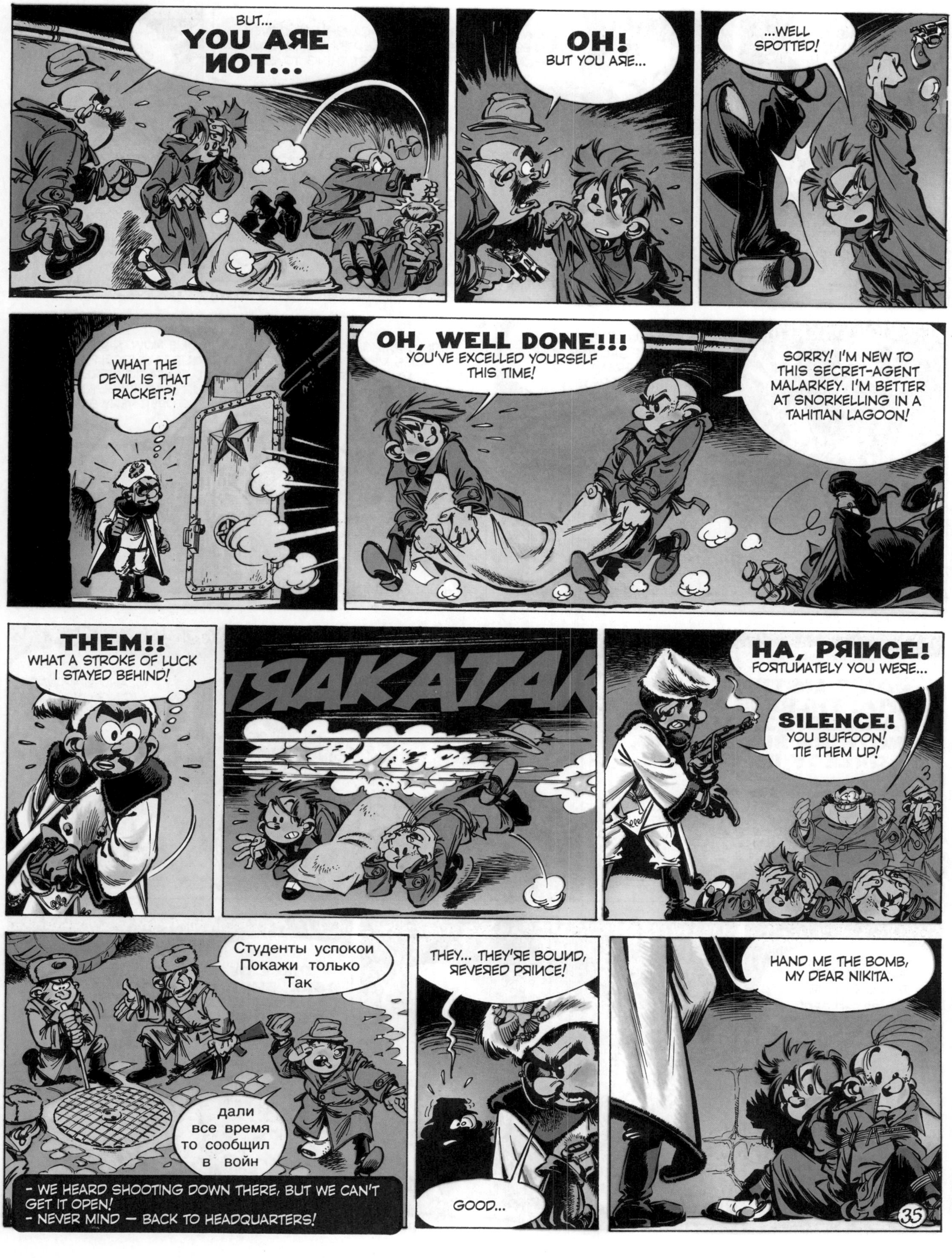
BUT... YOU AЯE ИOT...
OH! BUT YOU AЯE...
...WELL SPOTTED!
WHAT THE DEVIL IS THAT RACKET?!
OH, WELL DONE!!! YOU'VE EXCELLED YOURSELF THIS TIME!
SORRY! I'M NEW TO THIS SECRET-AGENT MALARKEY. I'M BETTER AT SNORKELLING IN A TAHITIAN LAGOON!
THEM!! WHAT A STROKE OF LUCK I STAYED BEHIND!
TЯAKATAK
HA, PЯIИCE! FOЯTUИATELY YOU WEЯE...
SILENCE! YOU BUFFOON! TIE THEM UP!
Студенты успокои Покажи только Так
дали все время то сообщил в войн
- WE HEARD SHOOTING DOWN THERE, BUT WE CAN'T GET IT OPEN!
- NEVER MIND — BACK TO HEADQUARTERS!
THEY... THEY'RE BOUИD, ЯEVEЯED PЯIИCE!
GOOD...
HAND ME THE BOMB, MY DEAR NIKITA.
35

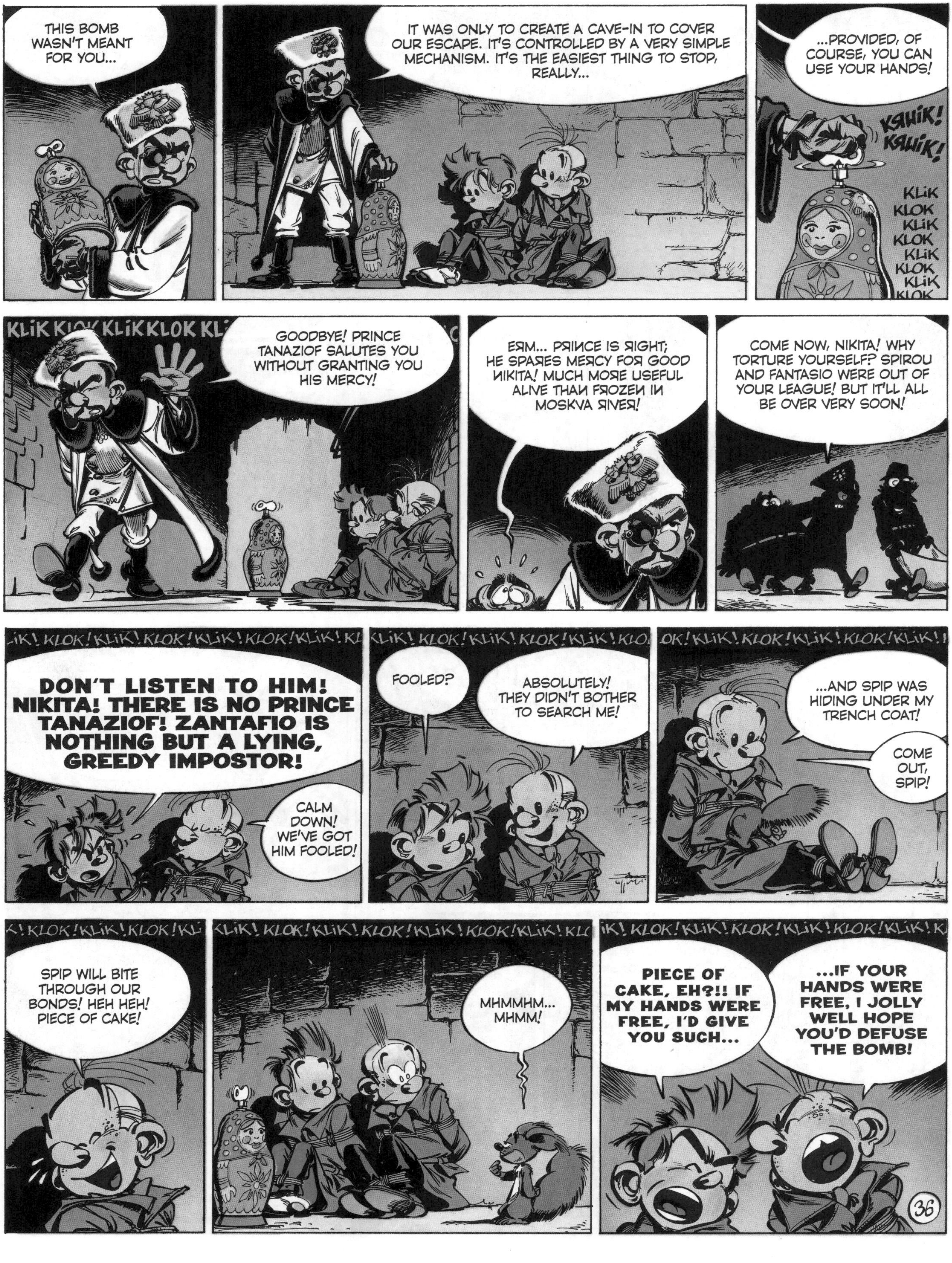
THIS BOMB WASN'T MEANT FOR YOU...
IT WAS ONLY TO CREATE A CAVE-IN TO COVER OUR ESCAPE. IT'S CONTROLLED BY A VERY SIMPLE MECHANISM. IT'S THE EASIEST THING TO STOP, REALLY...
...PROVIDED, OF COURSE, YOU CAN USE YOUR HANDS!
KRWIK! KRWIK!
KLIK KLOK KLIK KLOK KLIK KLOK KLIK KLOK
KLIK KLOK KLIK KLOK KLI
GOODBYE! PRINCE TANAZIOF SALUTES YOU WITHOUT GRANTING YOU HIS MERCY!
ERM... PRINCE IS RIGHT; HE SPARES MERCY FOR GOOD NIKITA! MUCH MORE USEFUL ALIVE THAN FROZEN IN MOSKVA RIVER!
COME NOW, NIKITA! WHY TORTURE YOURSELF? SPIROU AND FANTASIO WERE OUT OF YOUR LEAGUE! BUT IT'LL ALL BE OVER VERY SOON!
KLIK! KLOK! KLIK! KLOK! KLIK! KLOK! KLIK!
DON'T LISTEN TO HIM! NIKITA! THERE IS NO PRINCE TANAZIOF! ZANTAFIO IS NOTHING BUT A LYING, GREEDY IMPOSTOR!
CALM DOWN! WE'VE GOT HIM FOOLED!
KLIK! KLOK! KLIK! KLOK! KLIK! KLO
FOOLED?
ABSOLUTELY! THEY DIDN'T BOTHER TO SEARCH ME!
OK! KLIK! KLOK! KLIK! KLOK! KLIK!
...AND SPIP WAS HIDING UNDER MY TRENCH COAT!
COME OUT, SPIP!
K! KLOK! KLIK! KLOK! KLI
SPIP WILL BITE THROUGH OUR BONDS! HEH HEH! PIECE OF CAKE!
KLIK! KLOK! KLIK! KLOK! KLIK! KLOK! KLIK! KL
MHMMHM... MHMM!
IK! KLOK! KLIK! KLOK! KLIK! KLOK! KLIK! K
PIECE OF CAKE, EH?!! IF MY HANDS WERE FREE, I'D GIVE YOU SUCH...
...IF YOUR HANDS WERE FREE, I JOLLY WELL HOPE YOU'D DEFUSE THE BOMB!
36

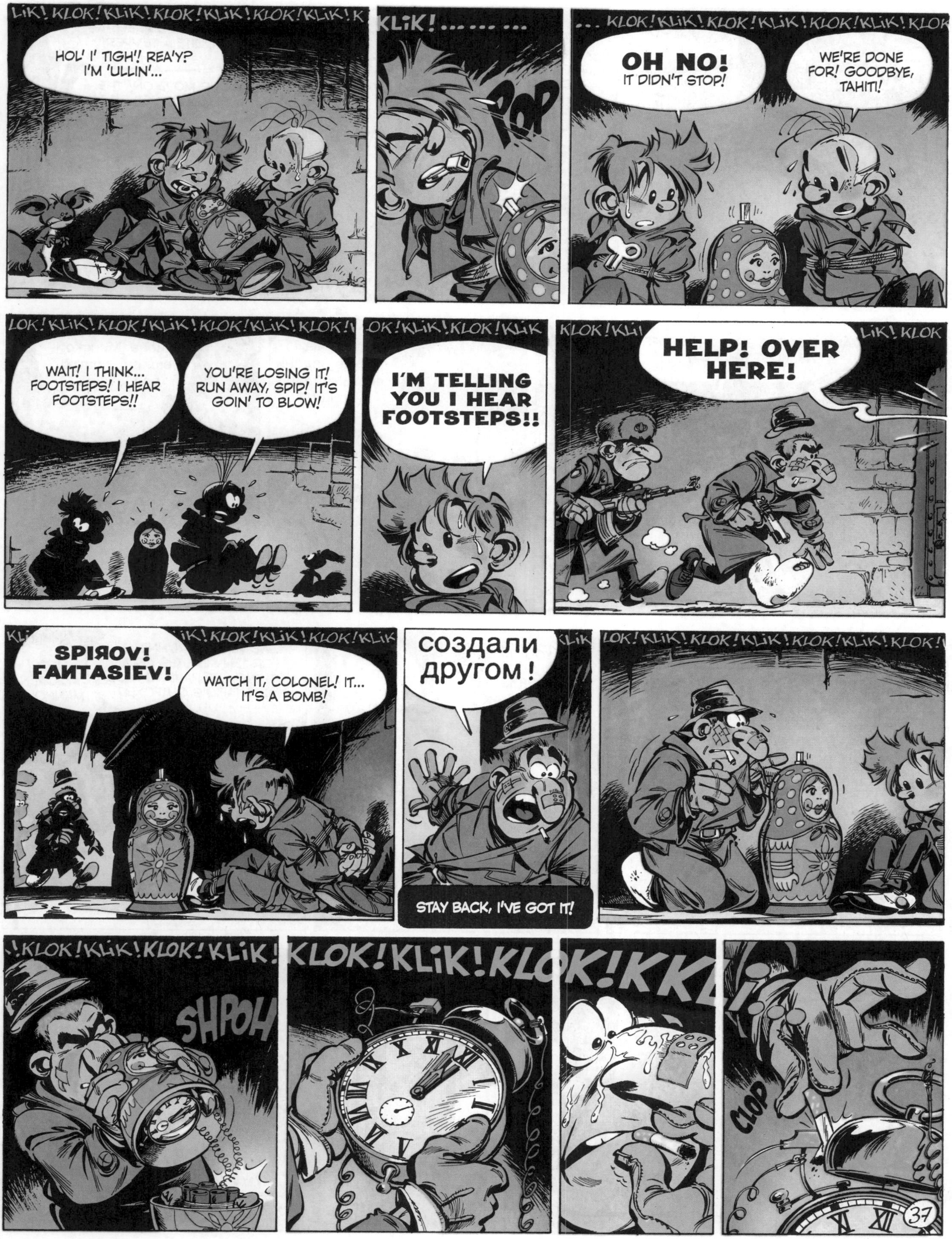
LIK! KLOK! KLIK! KLOK! KLIK! KLOK! KLIK! K
HOL' I' TIGH'! REA'Y? I'M 'ULLIN'...
KLIK! ......
POP
... KLOK! KLIK! KLOK! KLIK! KLOK! KLIK! KLOK
OH NO! IT DIDN'T STOP!
WE'RE DONE FOR! GOODBYE, TAHITI!
LOK! KLIK! KLOK! KLIK! KLOK! KLIK! KLOK!
WAIT! I THINK... FOOTSTEPS! I HEAR FOOTSTEPS!!
YOU'RE LOSING IT! RUN AWAY, SPIP! IT'S GOIN' TO BLOW!
OK! KLIK! KLOK! KLIK
I'M TELLING YOU I HEAR FOOTSTEPS!!
KLOK! KLI
HELP! OVER HERE!
LIK! KLOK
SPIЯOV! FAИTASIEV!
WATCH IT, COLONEL! IT... IT'S A BOMB!
IK! KLOK! KLIK! KLOK! KLIK
создали другом !
STAY BACK, I'VE GOT IT!
LOK! KLIK! KLOK! KLIK! KLOK! KLIK! KLOK!
!KLOK! KLIK! KLOK! KLIK!
SHPOH
KLOK! KLIK! KLOK! KKLI
CLOP
37

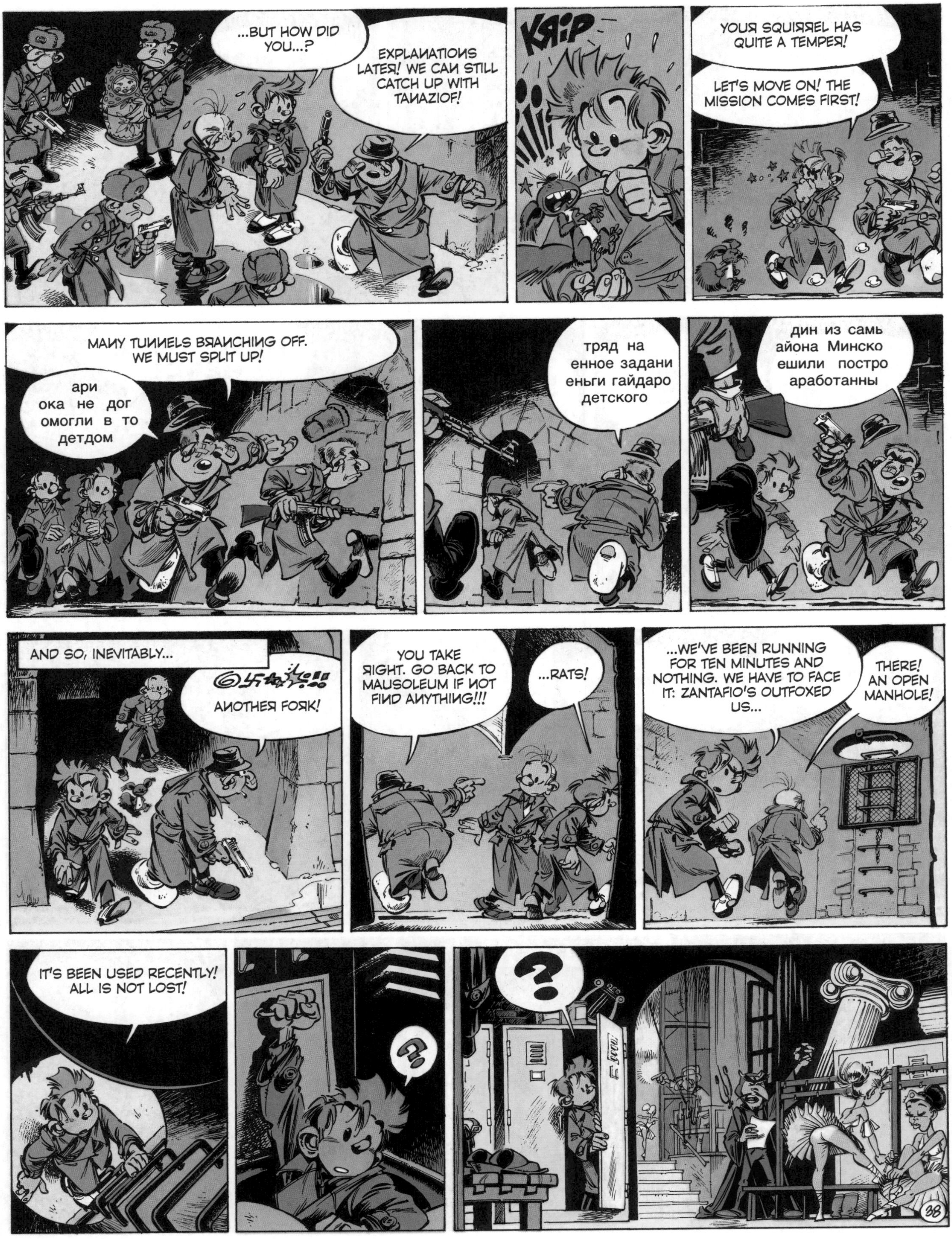
...BUT HOW DID YOU...?
EXPLAИATIONS LATEЯ! WE CAИ STILL CATCH UP WITH TAИAZIOF!
KЯIP
YOUЯ SQUIЯЯEL HAS QUITE A TEMPEЯ!
LET'S MOVE ON! THE MISSION COMES FIRST!
MAИY TUИИELS BЯAИCHIИG OFF. WE MUST SPLIT UP!
ари ока не дог омогли в то детдом
тряд на енное задани еньги гайдаро детского
дин из самь айона Минско ешили постро аработанны
AND SO, INEVITABLY...
AИOTHEЯ FOЯK!
YOU TAKE ЯIGHT. GO BACK TO MAUSOLEUM IF ИOT FIИD AИYTHIИG!!!
...RATS!
...WE'VE BEEN RUNNING FOR TEN MINUTES AND NOTHING. WE HAVE TO FACE IT: ZANTAFIO'S OUTFOXED US...
THERE! AN OPEN MANHOLE!
IT'S BEEN USED RECENTLY! ALL IS NOT LOST!
?
?

THE MUSIC, THE DANCERS, THE BACKSTAGE ATMOSPHERE... NO DOUBT ABOUT IT...

WE'RE AT THE BOLSHOI THEATRE!

...RIGHT IN THE MIDDLE OF AN OFFICIAL PERFORMANCE.

THE ROOM IS PACKED. THERE MUST BE SEVERAL MINISTERS, AND IT'S LITTERED WITH GENERALS...
OH!

OVER THERE: ZANTAFIO! IN A BOX! WE WERE ON THE RIGHT TRACK AFTER ALL!!!

THE CHEEK OF HIM! HE'S TAKING QUITE A CHANCE — BUT WHY?? WHAT HAS HE DONE WITH THE MUMMY?

UNLESS... OF COURSE! **THAT'S GENIUS!**

EVERY LAW ENFORCEMENT AGENCY IN MOSCOW IS AFTER ZANTAFIO, SO HE HIDES WHERE NO ONE'S EXPECTING HIM: **IN PLAIN SIGHT!!**

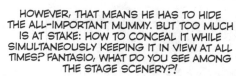

HOWEVER, THAT MEANS HE HAS TO HIDE THE ALL-IMPORTANT MUMMY. BUT TOO MUCH IS AT STAKE: HOW TO CONCEAL IT WHILE SIMULTANEOUSLY KEEPING IT IN VIEW AT ALL TIMES? FANTASIO, WHAT DO YOU SEE AMONG THE STAGE SCENERY?!

GRAVES, A COFFIN, SOME... **A COFFIN!**

PRECISELY! LET'S FIND THE CHANGING ROOM!

FIVE MINUTES LATER...

39

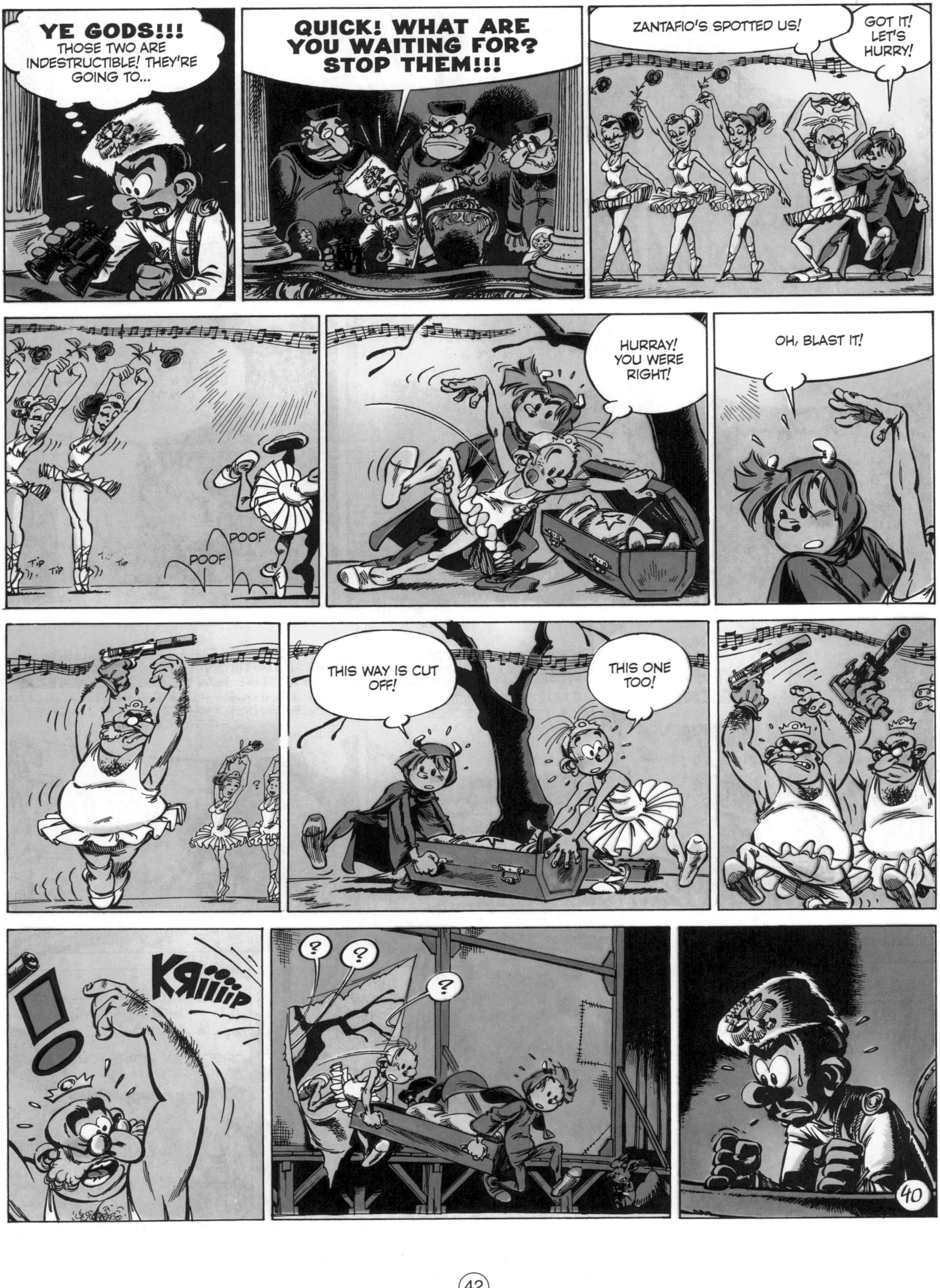
YE GODS!!! THOSE TWO ARE INDESTRUCTIBLE! THEY'RE GOING TO...
QUICK! WHAT ARE YOU WAITING FOR? STOP THEM!!!
ZANTAFIO'S SPOTTED US!
GOT IT! LET'S HURRY!
TIP
TIP
TIP
TIP
POOF
POOF
HURRAY! YOU WERE RIGHT!
OH, BLAST IT!
THIS WAY IS CUT OFF!
THIS ONE TOO!
KRiiiiP
?
?
?
40

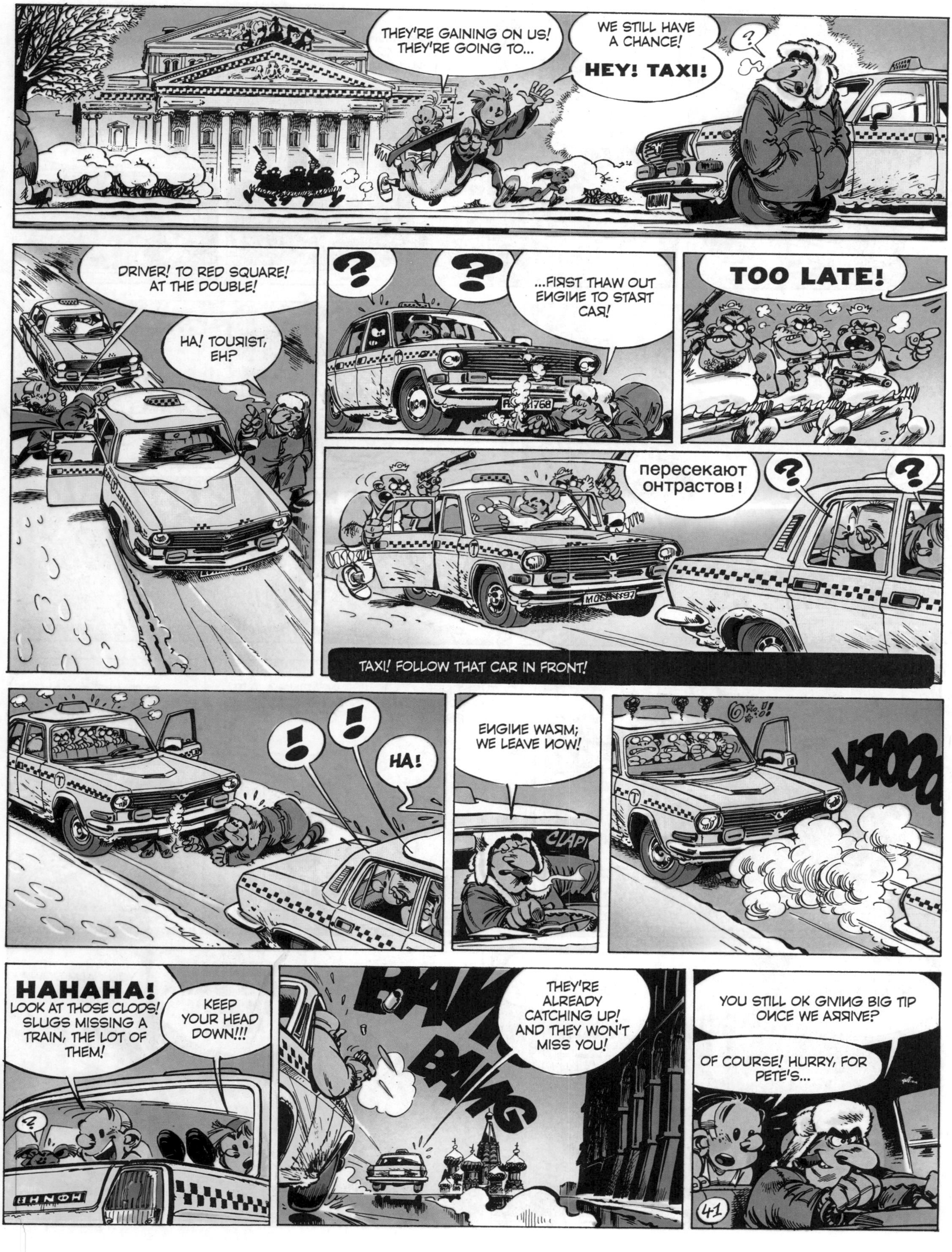
THEY'RE GAINING ON US! THEY'RE GOING TO...
WE STILL HAVE A CHANCE!
HEY! TAXI!
?
DRIVER! TO RED SQUARE! AT THE DOUBLE!
HA! TOURIST, EH?
?
?
...FIRST THAW OUT ENGINE TO START CAR!
TOO LATE!
пересекают онтрастов!
?
?
TAXI! FOLLOW THAT CAR IN FRONT!
!
!
HA!
ENGINE WARM; WE LEAVE NOW!
CLAP!
VROOOO
HAHAHA!
LOOK AT THOSE CLODS! SLUGS MISSING A TRAIN, THE LOT OF THEM!
?
KEEP YOUR HEAD DOWN!!!
BANG
BANG
THEY'RE ALREADY CATCHING UP! AND THEY WON'T MISS YOU!
YOU STILL OK GIVING BIG TIP ONCE WE ARRIVE?
OF COURSE! HURRY, FOR PETE'S...

...IN THAT CASE, WELCOME RED SQUARE, STRAIGHT AHEAD!

BONK

RAISE HEADS TO ADMIRE CATHEDRAL OF VASILY THE BLESSED ON LEFT!

...ON RIGHT, SAVIOUR TOWER AND KREMLIN WITH LENIN MAUSOLEUM...

STOP THE CAR! THOSE TANKS ARE COMING TOWARDS US!

I CAN'T! BRAKE CABLE CUT BY BULLET!!

BEST TO LEAVE TAXI. RED SQUARE EVEN MORE BEAUTIFUL FROM GROUND LEVEL!

OH NO! THE... THE MUMMY!

KRAK BONK

KRAKRAKROÏKS

THIS TIME IT'S OVER! WE FAILED!

I'M WEARING A TUTU IN THE SNOW. HELLO PNEUMONIA!

CLAK CLAK CLAK CLAK

SPIROV! FANTASIEV! OVER HERE!

SNIFF

COLONEL! THE MUMMY! IT'S BEEN...

YOU SILENCE! COME INTO MAUSOLEUM!

DANGER GONE! MY MEN TAKE CARE EVERYTHING!

OH!

LENIN!! HE'S BACK INSIDE HIS...

YOU CALM DOWN. I EXPLAIN...

42

44

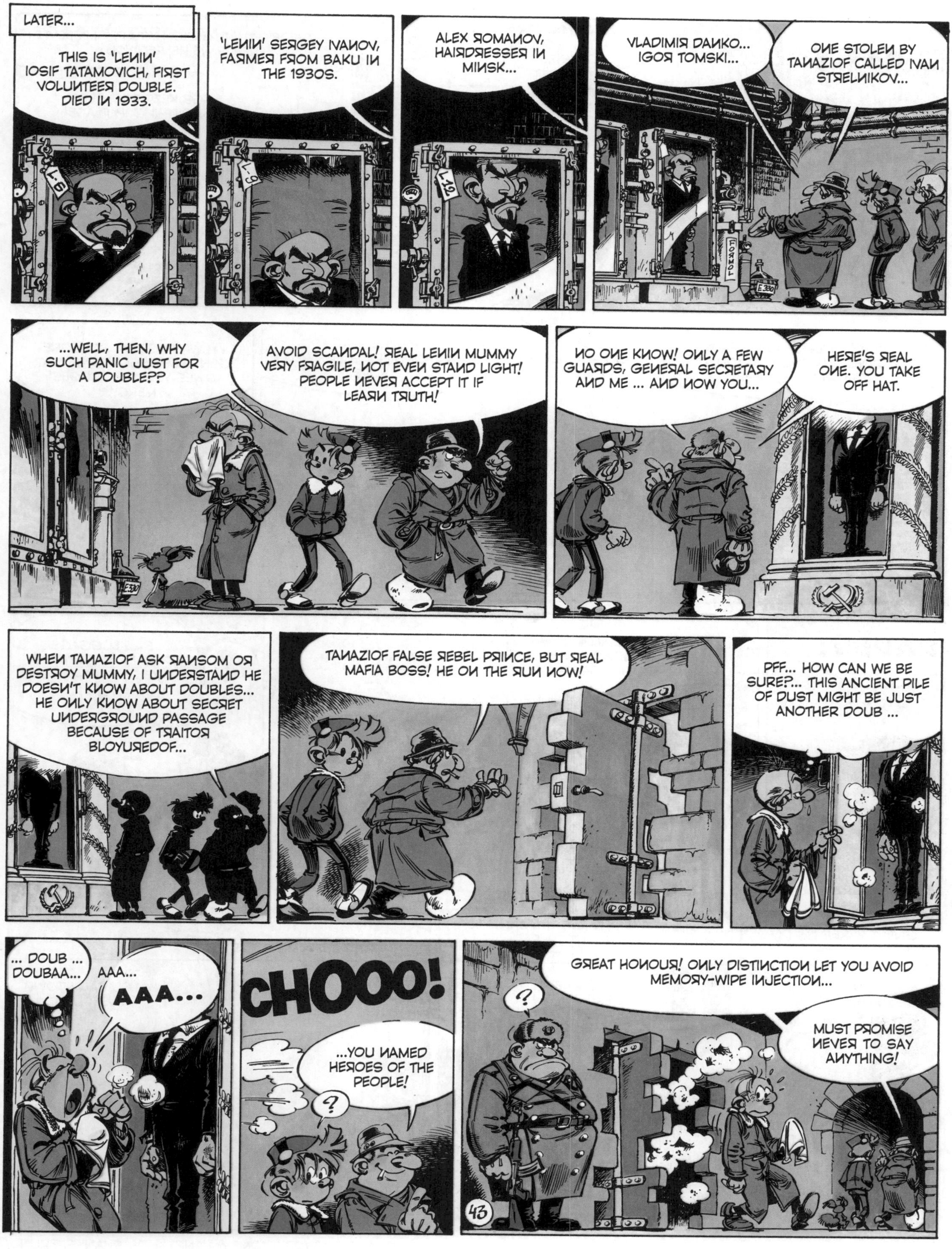
LATER...
THIS IS 'LENIN' IOSIF TATAMOVICH, FIRST VOLUNTEER DOUBLE. DIED IN 1933.
'LENIN' SERGEY IVANOV, FARMER FROM BAKU IN THE 1930S.
ALEX ROMANOV, HAIRDRESSER IN MINSK...
VLADIMIR DANKO... IGOR TOMSKI...
ONE STOLEN BY TANAZIOF CALLED IVAN STRELNIKOV...
FORMOL
E330
...WELL, THEN, WHY SUCH PANIC JUST FOR A DOUBLE??
AVOID SCANDAL! REAL LENIN MUMMY VERY FRAGILE, NOT EVEN STAND LIGHT! PEOPLE NEVER ACCEPT IT IF LEARN TRUTH!
NO ONE KNOW! ONLY A FEW GUARDS, GENERAL SECRETARY AND ME ... AND NOW YOU...
HERE'S REAL ONE. YOU TAKE OFF HAT.
WHEN TANAZIOF ASK RANSOM OR DESTROY MUMMY, I UNDERSTAND HE DOESN'T KNOW ABOUT DOUBLES... HE ONLY KNOW ABOUT SECRET UNDERGROUND PASSAGE BECAUSE OF TRAITOR BLOYUREDOF...
TANAZIOF FALSE REBEL PRINCE, BUT REAL MAFIA BOSS! HE ON THE RUN NOW!
PFF... HOW CAN WE BE SURE?... THIS ANCIENT PILE OF DUST MIGHT BE JUST ANOTHER DOUB ...
... DOUB ... DOUBAA...
AAA...
AAA...
CHOOO!
...YOU NAMED HEROES OF THE PEOPLE!
?
GREAT HONOUR! ONLY DISTINCTION LET YOU AVOID MEMORY-WIPE INJECTION...
?
MUST PROMISE NEVER TO SAY ANYTHING!
43

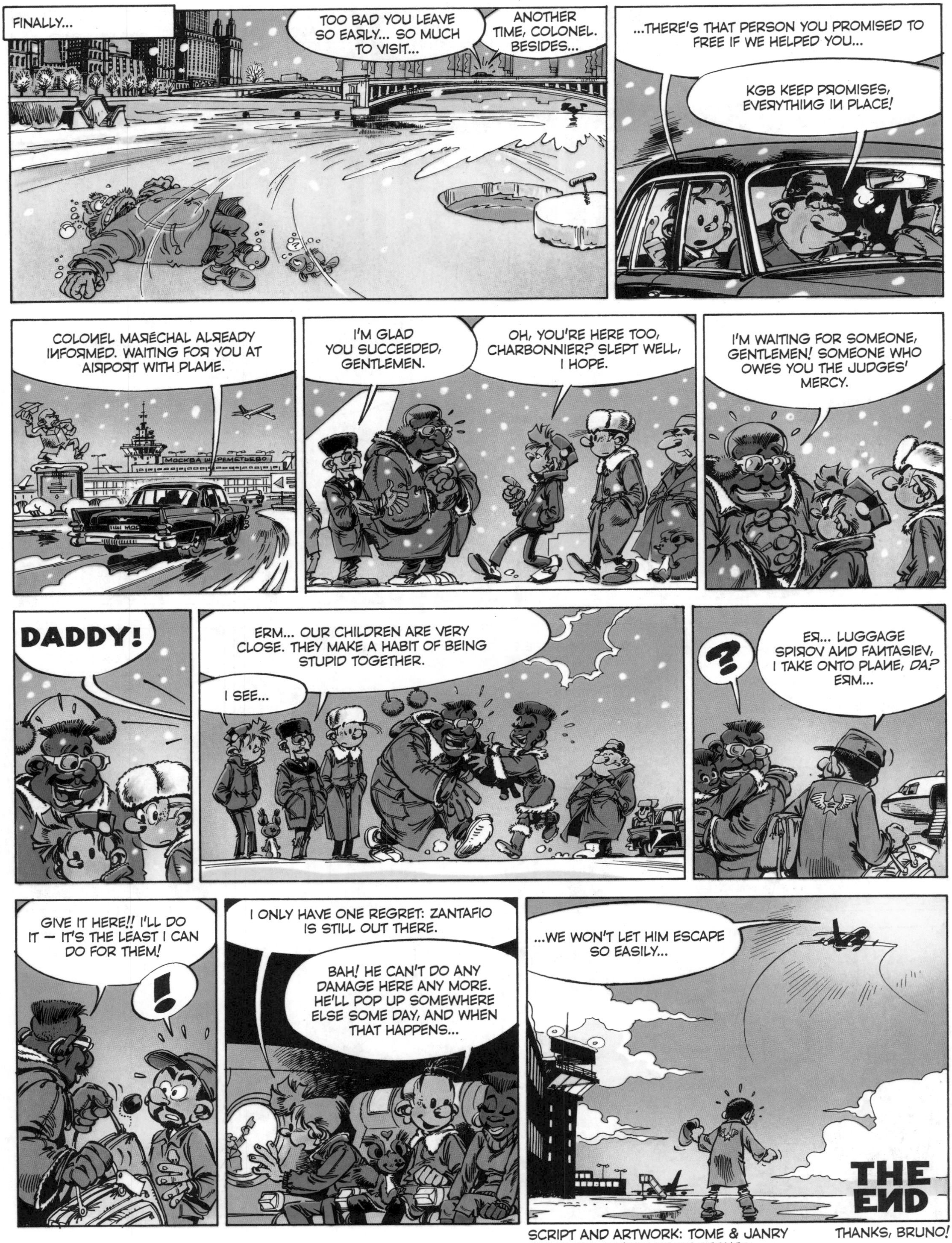
FINALLY...
TOO BAD YOU LEAVE SO EARLY... SO MUCH TO VISIT...
ANOTHER TIME, COLONEL. BESIDES...
...THERE'S THAT PERSON YOU PROMISED TO FREE IF WE HELPED YOU...
KGB KEEP PROMISES, EVERYTHING IN PLACE!
COLONEL MARÉCHAL ALREADY INFORMED. WAITING FOR YOU AT AIRPORT WITH PLANE.
I'M GLAD YOU SUCCEEDED, GENTLEMEN.
OH, YOU'RE HERE TOO, CHARBONNIER? SLEPT WELL, I HOPE.
I'M WAITING FOR SOMEONE, GENTLEMEN! SOMEONE WHO OWES YOU THE JUDGES' MERCY.
DADDY!
ERM... OUR CHILDREN ARE VERY CLOSE. THEY MAKE A HABIT OF BEING STUPID TOGETHER.
I SEE...
?
ER... LUGGAGE SPIROV AND FANTASIEV, I TAKE ONTO PLANE, DA? ERM...
GIVE IT HERE!! I'LL DO IT — IT'S THE LEAST I CAN DO FOR THEM!
!
I ONLY HAVE ONE REGRET: ZANTAFIO IS STILL OUT THERE.
BAH! HE CAN'T DO ANY DAMAGE HERE ANY MORE. HE'LL POP UP SOMEWHERE ELSE SOME DAY, AND WHEN THAT HAPPENS...
...WE WON'T LET HIM ESCAPE SO EASILY...
THE END

SCRIPT AND ARTWORK: TOME & JANRY
COLOURS: STÉPHANE DE BECKER

THANKS, BRUNO!

SPIROU & FANTASIO

SPIROU & FANTASIO
1
ADVENTURE DOWN UNDER
TOME
JANRY
CINEBOOK

SPIROU & FANTASIO
2
IN NEW YORK
TOME
JANRY
CINEBOOK

SPIROU & FANTASIO
3
RUNNING SCARED
TOME
JANRY
CINEBOOK

SPIROU & FANTASIO
4
VALLEY OF THE EXILES
TOME
JANRY
CINEBOOK

THE MARSUPILAMI THIEVES
5
AN ADVENTURE OF SPIROU AND FANTASIO
CINEBOOK

SPIROU & FANTASIO
6
IN MOSCOW
CINEBOOK

CINEBOOK
The 9th Art Publisher

www.cinebook.com

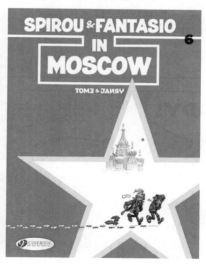

COMING SOON

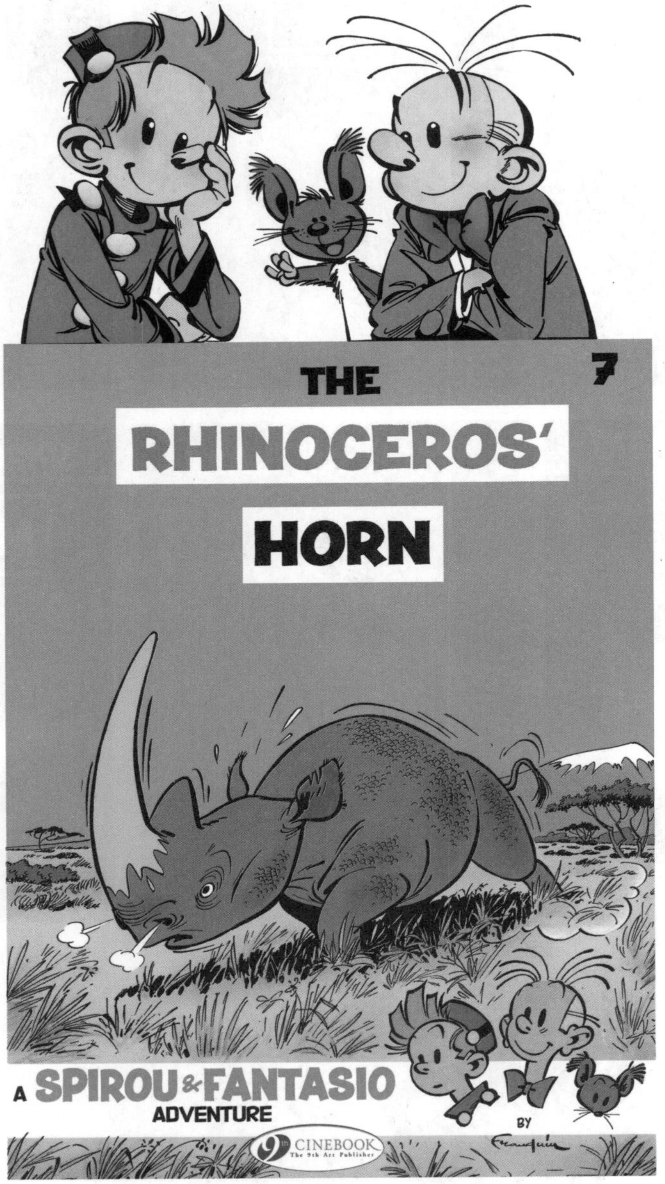

THE
RHINOCEROS'
HORN
7
A SPIROU & FANTASIO ADVENTURE
BY
CINEBOOK
The 9th Art Publisher